"I Knew You Were What I Wanted from the Moment I Saw You."

He drew Melora into his arms and she went unresisting. When he kissed her she no longer tried to think. This was something she had wanted and dreamed about. She could not question this moment with his arms around her and his cheek rough against her own. She knew he was going much too fast, but she felt too breathlessly happy to be bothered with words.

He gave her a last kiss and then took her hand. "We'd better go back before they send out a search party. . . ."

D0037328

The Fire
and the Gold

by
Phyllis A. Whitney

A SIGNET BOOK
NEW AMERICAN LIBRARY
TIMES MIRROR

Library of Congress Catalog Card Number: 56-5324

"The Ballad of the Hyde Street Grip" by Gelett Burgess, on pp. 189-190 first appeared in *A Gage of Youth* and is reprinted by permission of Miss Louise Andrews.

This is an authorized reprint of a hardcover book published by Thomas E. Crowell Company, Inc. The hardcover edition was published simultaneously in Canada by Fitzhenry & Whiteside Limited, Toronto.

SIGNET, SIGNET CLASSICS, SIGNETTE, MENTOR AND PLUME BOOKS are published by The New American Library, Inc., 1301 Avenue of the Americas, New York, New York 10019

FIRST PRINTING, JANUARY, 1974

1 2 3 4 5 6 7 8 9

PRINTED IN THE UNITED STATES OF AMERICA

To my mother
who first showed me
San Francisco

Contents

A
DIAMOND SOLITAIRE

The train, whistling impatiently as it sped through the April morning, sent black smoke billowing in its wake. For the hundredth time in the nearly three days of the trip west from Chicago, Melora Cranby lifted her book and dusted gritty cinders from the gray broadcloth skirt of her tailor-made suit. She wished the journey were over. Not that there wouldn't be problems waiting for her in San Francisco, but now she wanted to get home and face them.

The fact that they were problems of her own making caused her to feel all the more uncomfortable. She turned a page of her novel by Rudyard Kipling and realized that she hadn't understood a word she'd been reading.

In the green plush Pullman seat opposite, Mrs. Forrest regarded her with disturbing curiosity. Melora had gone east to Chicago to attend the marriage of a cousin. As an old friend of the family, Nell Forrest had been happy to pick her up on her own way home from New York to San Francisco. Even in this enlightened year of 1906, with the old century behind them, it would scarcely be suitable for a well brought up girl of nineteen to travel alone on so long a trip.

But Melora could have wished for a less curious companion. Mrs. Forrest liked people and she was talkative. Her large feathered hat bobbed energetically to emphasize her words, and not since Chicago had she given up her effort to penetrate the guard Melora tried to hold against her.

The main focus of her interest was plainly the fine solitaire which sparkled on the engagement finger of Melora's left hand. Mrs. Forrest probably expected her to be bubbling with anticipation over seeing Quent Seymour again. The whole family had been delighted over this engagement, yet Melora's gray eyes were unsmiling, her lips fixed in a determined line as she thought of how upset her mother was going to be when she knew the truth.

Mrs. Forrest placed her handsome alligator handbag on the seat beside her and leaned forward to tap Melora's knee. "Did you enjoy Chicago so much that you dislike going home?"

Melora looked up from the book she was pretending to read. "Oh, no. I love San Francisco. I've been homesick for it."

"Mm," said Mrs. Forrest doubtfully. "I suppose you'll be impatient for your own wedding now, after all this excitement at your cousin's. Your sister Cora must be as thrilled as you over the prospect of all the parties and showers and preparations. Have you set the date yet?"

"Not yet," Melora said a trifle quickly. "I didn't want—that is, Mama agreed that it would be better to wait until Papa's ship gets home from the Orient sometime in June before we make an announcement. We'd like to—to talk everything over with him."

Mrs. Forrest looked as though she wondered about that. And well she might. Adelina Cranby would certainly have consulted Captain Cranby every step of the way if she'd had any doubt about this marriage. But Melora knew—and so did Mrs. Forrest—that Quentin Seymour had always been regarded as an ideal match. The Seymours were old friends with a mansion on Nob Hill and all that bonanza money behind them. To say nothing of Will Seymour's profitable insurance business. It must have seemed to Mrs. Forrest that there was no possible reason for this delay in making an announcement.

Melora gave up pretending to look at the book. She twisted the ring on her finger and stared uneasily at the changing scene which brought them always nearer to the Oakland mole, where the ferries docked. Sometimes she wished she were more like her sixteen-year-old sister Cora, who took things gayly in her stride and had thus far had little reason for unhappy introspection. Alec too, her small brother who was only eight, had the ability to storm his problems and solve them in a headlong fashion that had been foreign to Melora, even as a child.

Perhaps if she gave Mrs. Forrest some inkling of what was wrong—tried to talk a little, instead of sitting here resisting her friendly interest—?

She spoke suddenly without shifting the direction of her gaze from the window. "When you were young, didn't you ever want to get away? I mean didn't you want to sail the seas and meet people who were different from the everyday people around you? Didn't you ever want to *do* something, or *be* somebody? Something or somebody a long way from what Nob Hill stands for."

"Well!" said Mrs. Forrest, decidedly taken aback. "What is it you would like to be, Melora?"

"That's the trouble—I don't know." The answer certainly didn't lie in marrying Quent Seymour and going to live on Nob Hill. "I've wondered about the sort of life you've lived. Mama says you're frightfully independent and you go anywhere you want as you choose."

"No one does exactly what he chooses," said Mrs. Forrest. "But don't forget that I'm an old woman with a grown-up son. I've earned the right to do as I please to some extent. Besides, when my husband was alive and a state senator, we lived an unusual sort of existence and met all sorts of people. I suppose I still do, with my son Howard editing *Mission Bells Magazine* and inviting so many professional people to our home."

Her home, Melora knew, was a sumptuous family suite on an upper residential floor of the Palace Hotel. Melora had been there to tea more than once with her mother and found it a place where interesting people talked about fascinating topics and one had a tantalizing sense of the outside world coming in. But how could she ever taste the outside world, except through books, within the tight little walls of her mother's San Francisco? Papa had it, and talked about it, but his daughter could hardly run away to sea. Gran had had it too.

"Grandmother lived a different sort of life." Melora put her thought into words.

Grandmother Melora Bonner, for whom she had been named, had lived in Virginia City when the Comstock Lode was in full bonanza. Gran often spoke of how hard she had worked in her mother's boarding house in the days before she married Henry Bonner. She had worked after marrying Henry too, because he had been a nobody until his luck came in and he practically rolled in silver wealth. Then he'd been able to build a fine home with a view of the bay out on Washington Street in San Francisco. A home that was now leased to tenants, much to her mother's distress.

"You mustn't forget," Mrs. Forrest reminded her,

"that your grandmother belongs to an old southern family and lived her girlhood on a South Carolina plantation. Your mother feels you have a good deal of family to live up to."

"But the Civil War changed all that," Melora pointed out. "Grandmother's family fortune was wiped out and she moved away with her father and mother when the carpetbaggers came in. I don't think she holds so much with that fine-old-name sort of thing some of Mama's friends dote on."

Besides, she thought, when Grandfather had died with most of his fortune lost in a crash, they'd had little money left to speak of. Now there was just Papa's salary as captain of a merchant vessel, and Papa preferred to live quietly in an unfashionable little house not far from Market Street. Mama had really hated that. But she kept her society friends and she was ambitious for her daughters. Almost frighteningly ambitious, Melora thought uncomfortably.

Unexpectedly the train had begun to slow its rocking pace and Melora glanced out the window with a start. There was supposed to be no scheduled stop before Oakland and they were due there around noon— an hour or so away.

"It's a small station of some sort," Mrs. Forrest said, putting her head out the window as the train halted at a wooden platform with a shed beside it. "Look at the people! I wonder what's happening."

She tried to catch the attention of a small boy who ran beneath her window to join the crowd near the engine, but he paid no attention, so she settled back to wait.

"I wish we could have reached home a day or two earlier, Melora," she said. "I'd have given anything to hear Caruso and Fremstad sing *Carmen* last night at the Opera House."

Melora made no comment, lost again in her own

musings. She twisted the diamond on her finger once more, thinking of Quentin Seymour. He had always been part of her life, as familiar to her everyday scene as a pair of old shoes. She smiled to herself, wondering how Quent would feel about such a comparison. Probably he wouldn't be surprised. Most likely he regarded her as an old-shoe sort of person too.

How do I love thee, she thought in wry amusement and yearned again for the unknown, the unfamiliar. Elizabeth Barrett Browning had lived a romance and adventure even though she'd been an invalid. She hadn't been shoved into a make-believe engagement with a boy who hardly ever opened a book and who had kicked her on the shins most ungallantly at the age of six.

The trouble was that Quent's mother and Melora's had always been close friends. From the time Melora was fourteen the two had begun thrusting son and daughter together most annoyingly. But nothing would have happened if it hadn't been for that lunatic idea of Quent's. She and Cora and Mama had been invited by the Seymours to attend a performance at the open-air Greek theater in Berkeley, and on the ferry coming home Mrs. Seymour and her own mother had sent Quent and Melora off to walk the deck by themselves. Melora had squirmed over the knowing looks that passed between the two women and Quent had been quick to see her expression.

"Look here, Melora," he said with mischief alight in his eyes, "there's a way to end this matchmaking business and get ourselves some freedom at the same time. That is, if you're game."

A pale half-moon was shining over San Francisco Bay that night and its light touched Quent's fair hair to gold as he leaned on the rail at her side.

"What are you talking about?" she asked, her eyes

on the tiered lights that marched up the hills of the city, and shone in its tall downtown buildings.

"We could get engaged," he said bluntly. "That would put a stop to all this. They could just relax and sit back and feel their job was done. Then you and I could have some fun and not be so self-conscious because we know what they're up to."

She'd forgotten the beautiful city and turned to look at him directly. "Quent! If you think for one moment that I'd—"

He waved his hands at her. "Don't be so hasty, lady. I'm not proposing marriage. Goodness knows, when I marry I want a gal with some mystery and allure. Not somebody who's been practically a sister all my life. I'm only suggesting a way to put a stop to the matchmaking. I wouldn't even have to buy a ring, since my grandmother willed me hers to be used when I got engaged. It's a beaut too. You can flash it under everyone's nose and your mother will be tickled pink."

Somehow his words had annoyed her. Particularly the part about her lacking mystery and allure.

He sensed her annoyance at once. "Aw, Missy M'lory, don't be mad. You know I like you fine. You've got heaps of sense and gumption. And you don't chatter all the time."

"Missy M'lory" was what Quong Sam, the Cranbys' Chinese cook, always called her and it made her smile as Quent used it.

But she remained unmollified. It was like Quent to be irresponsible about such things.

"You don't know mothers," she pointed out. "Give them a notion of this kind and they'd start notices to the papers, announcements, parties—goodness knows what. And there'd be the showers and the trousseau and the business of setting the date. We'd be in such deep water we'd never swim out. No thank you, I don't want to go through all that."

Quent stared disconsolately at the lights across the bay. "I suppose you're right. I didn't think of all that part of it."

"You could go out with other girls," Melora suggested.

"You think I don't? But all my mother does is make odious comparisons. With you. Never have I seen a more single-minded woman." He looked at Melora suddenly, grinning. "Why can't I see you the way she does? It might simplify everything."

"It would not!" said Melora flatly, and he laughed. "At least," she went on, "I'll be escaping for a while."

"You mean because of your trip to Chicago? Lucky you. But I'll still be here for them to work on. Say—maybe that's the answer!"

She listened then, tempted in spite of herself. The plea, he explained, would be that since Melora was going away shortly, no formal announcement should be made until her return. Even better, let the whole thing remain quiet until her father came home in June. If they could sell this idea to their mothers, perhaps they could be left alone for a few months. At the end of that time they could quietly "break" the engagement and the matchmaking would have to stop for good. It was really a masterful idea, Quent insisted.

In the end Melora gave in, not altogether convinced, and far from comfortable about the deception involved, but swayed by Quent's enthusiasm and by her own restlessness and desire for a change.

When they rejoined their mothers they had to endure a good deal of gushing. But after the first excitement died down it had seemed as though the thing might work out and even be rather amusing. It hadn't been easy to persuade two such delighted women to suppress their desire for immediate publicity, but Quent and Melora had managed to bargain. It was to be a quiet engagement for right now, or nothing, they said. So both women had reluctantly consented.

The one duty Melora disliked most was writing about it to her father, as Mama had instructed her to do. She had always been completely honest with her father, and since she liked to put words on paper, her letters were usually long ones. But this letter had been hard.

After tearing up three attempts, Melora had wanted to set the whole thing down exactly as it had happened. But she suspected that her father would not approve, and more than anything she wanted his approval and love. So in the end she had written mostly about other matters, and at the very close, in a postscript, she had put down a single sentence: "Quentin Seymour and I are engaged." That was true enough. The letter had gone off to him six weeks before she left for her visit to Chicago, and she rather dreaded his answer.

In Chicago she'd had time to think and she meant to end the whole silly performance the minute she could get hold of Quent and talk some sense into him. In spite of any "bargain" Mama was taking this seriously, and there was already sewing and trousseau preparing going on. It had to be stopped before it became more than Melora could deal with.

Outside on the train platform the crowd was increasing and the noise and confusion brought Melora back to the present. The passengers were growing curious and some of the men had left the train to join in the excited talk on the platform. Obviously something unusual had happened.

Once more Mrs. Forrest put her head out the window and spoke to a man running by. "What's happened?" she called. "What's wrong?"

The fellow stopped, breathing hard. "Dunno for sure. Big earthquake, I guess. Looks like the whole bay area around San Francisco's been wiped out."

Mrs. Forrest gasped and sat back in her seat. Melora stared at her, shocked, but not really believing.

"Don't let's get excited," Mrs. Forrest said. "San Francisco's had earthquakes before and it's still standing. People always exaggerate. Why, this will just be something to write about in that diary you're always bringing out. Stay right here, dear, I'm going to see what I can learn about what's really happened."

She rose and went down the aisle, the feathers on her large hat waving a little at the swiftness of her passage, her heavy skirt brushing past the seats. Melora pinned her own little sailor hat more securely lest the wind send it soaring, and leaned out the window herself.

The group down the platform seemed to be having a considerable disagreement. Some of the men were shouting and waving at the engineer and he was shouting and waving back. Once Melora caught the word "Fire!" but everyone was making so much noise that it wasn't possible to get any sense out of the talk. She looked around anxiously as Mrs. Forrest returned to her seat. Her calm manner was reassuring.

"There does seem to have been an earthquake in San Francisco early this morning," she said. "Unfortunately communications have broken down. The only news that's coming through is from cities outside the earthquake range. There's a rumor that a fire has started in the city, but I don't think we need to worry about that. Our fire department is one of the best in the country and it will have matters under control by now."

The train gave a jerk that threw them back in their seats, and began to chug its way out of the little station. On the platform the excited throng stood waving them off. Some few newcomers had boarded the train, evidently wanting to go on to the disaster section.

In a few moments the conductor came through and

announced that the train would continue to Oakland as scheduled, since there appeared to be no reason not to enter that city.

The remaining time into Oakland seemed to stretch out endlessly. Of course everything would be all right, Melora told herself. It was as Mrs. Forrest said—people were ready to scream murder when someone was pricked by a pin.

They got their suitcases from under the seats, since the porter had his hands full with demands, and lined up in the aisle so they might be among the first to leave the car when the train reached the mole. Glimpses out the windows were both reassuring and troubling. There had, indeed, been an earthquake of some violence. You could see that a number of chimneys were down, and here and there a wall had collapsed. But most of the houses stood with no visible damage, though one could imagine how bric-a-brac must have been flung about within.

As she stood in the aisle behind Mrs. Forrest, clinging to the back of a seat, Melora found herself thinking of her father's third-floor study at home. A long-time Chinese friend of Captain Andrew Cranby had given him a beautiful and valuable statue of the Goddess of Mercy, Kwan Yin. Melora could see the golden-faced statue clearly on its shelf in the study and she hoped the precious porcelain figure had not been damaged.

The train jolted and halted again, then jerked to a complete stop. The journey was over. They could see at once that the train sheds were crowded with excited people—people who seemed ready to force themselves aboard the train even before the current passengers left it.

Mrs. Forrest held her suitcase firmly in one hand and grasped Melora's wrist with the other. "Don't let anyone come between us. We mustn't be separated.

Let's get into the open and find out what's really going on."

They had to struggle through a crowd that fairly pushed them back into the train. Mrs. Forrest's hat was tilted sideways and she had no free hand with which to right it. Melora's small sailor, well pinned, fared better, but she was glad to move in the comparative safety of Mrs. Forrest's large wake.

Everywhere now they heard the word "fire" and on the air there was a faint smell of smoke drifting across the bay. Once in the open they stumbled into a cleared space away from the crowd's path and stood where they could look across the bay to the city. Billowing black columns of smoke poured upward from several parts of the area south of Market Street. And even at this distance they could see clouds of white smoke too, and the flash of flame.

"Looks like there is a bit of a fire," Mrs. Forrest said. "May take the fire department a while to get it under control after all." But her voice shook a little as she spoke.

"What are we going to do?" Melora asked.

Mrs. Forrest took a deep breath, seemed to steady herself. "Do? Why, we'll go across, of course. The fire's all in one location—you can see the rest of the city is all right. The main thing is to rejoin our families and do whatever they do. Don't you agree?"

"Of course," said Melora faintly. "But do you think the ferries are running?"

Mrs. Forrest gestured with one hand, while she held her hat with the other. "Of course they are. You can see one bringing in a boatland of people now. Probably they'll go back for more, and we'll get on board."

But it was not to be as simple as that, as Mrs. Forrest discovered when she and Melora tried to move in the direction of the ferry slip. A man leaving the boat told them that General Funston had sent troops in from the Presidio and that only authorized persons were being allowed to disembark at the Ferry Building.

"People are coming out, not going in," he said. "You're headed the wrong way!"

Across the bay the City of St. Francis still gleamed upon its hills even as it wrapped itself in a pall of smoke.

2

THE
FLAMING CITY

Mrs. Forrest was not one to give in easily when an obstacle was placed in her path. Her determination to rejoin her son in their suite at the Palace was as strong as ever.

"But what if he has left by now?" Melora asked hesitantly, wondering if her own family too might be coming out of the city while she followed Mrs. Forrest in.

The older woman shook her head. "Nonsense! Howard isn't one to give up the ship. His magazine is published over there. Besides, he's like me—San Francisco bred and born and he'd stand by when there was trouble. Melora, you sit right here on these suitcases and don't budge an inch. I'm going to see what I can find out."

She was off before Melora could object. There was nothing to do but seat herself on the two suitcases and wait. It was hard to believe in what was happening. The morning was cold but beautiful. The sun was brilliant over Oakland, where drifting smoke had not yet obscured its rays.

The refugee group came straggling up from the ferry, wearing every possible assortment of dress and undress, carrying what worldly goods they could save on their backs and in their arms. Watching them, Melora felt somehow remote and unconcerned, as if she were attending a play. *Her* family could be taking no part in this. She had the quiet conviction that at home Quong Sam would be preparing to serve lunch and everything would be as usual. But as the refugees stumbled past she caught snatches of conversation that were hardly reassuring.

"The quake started it—lamps and stoves in those wooden shacks south of Market . . ."

"Earthquake broke the water mains . . ."

"Fire chief's been killed . . ."

"Not a drop of water to fight it with . . ."

"Nope, it's not across Market yet . . ."

Melora sat on the suitcases, watching, listening. This was all something out of a bad dream. Market Street was wide. Surely the fire couldn't leap Market. But with no water . . . Panic began to rise in her—a contagion that fairly oozed from the crowds surging past her. It was all she could do to suppress an urge to rush aimlessly off among the refugees.

It was a relief to see Mrs. Forrest coming back. Her graying pompadour straggled in wisps about her forehead, but the feathers on her big hat waved like flags of triumph.

"They still remember the Senator in these parts," she said. "And of course money talks a bit too. There's a little tugboat that came to the mole with some refugees. Its captain is willing to take us across. We'll go around by Fisherman's Wharf, far away from the fire. Then I'll get downtown somehow. I'll leave you at your house and go on to the Palace." Mrs. Forrest plainly had her teeth in this and she was not the deviating sort.

"Have you heard about the water mains breaking?" Melora asked. "They're saying there's no water to fight the fire. And the Palace is on the wrong side of Market."

Mrs. Forrest reached for her suitcase without a pause. "The Palace will be the safest place in town. The hotel's not dependent on the city for water. There's a 630,000-gallon water supply right under the Grand Lounge. Come along now. We'll have to get rid of these suitcases. Goodness knows how far we may have to walk."

It was good to spring into some sort of action. Once more they crowded into the station and found the checking desk deserted. Mrs. Forrest shoved their suitcases across the counter and dusted her hands.

"They'll be safe enough here. Our names are on them. That boat won't wait for us forever."

They hurried down to the dock and clambered down a ladder, clinging to their long hampering skirts with one hand and the rungs with the other. Below them the little boat bounced gently.

As the tug nosed off across the bay, Melora and Mrs. Forrest sat in its small cabin, peering through smeary windows. Now they could see the fire clearly and the area it covered was appallingly large. At the foot of Market Street the white tower of the Ferry Building stood up squarely, silhouetted against the smoke and flame behind it.

The tugboat captain said he had some grub aboard and suggested that they'd better eat hearty while they had the chance. They accepted his cold baked beans and rye bread gratefully and ate while they watched the spreading canopy of smoke over the shore. The sun was dimming now in the haze and the smell of the burning grew stronger.

Melora's peaceful imaginings of her family having lunch had faded. She was thankful for the presence of

Quong Sam in her father's house. For as long as she could remember he had met emergencies with more presence of mind than anyone except Gran. Once Gran could have been counted on to take charge, but lately she had seemed increasingly frail, and the family had worried about her. How awful if she should now be thrust out on the street, forced into a hurrying, frightened crowd.

There was a sudden flash of light over near Market Street, followed by a puff of white smoke. The clap of the explosion reached them seconds later.

"Something's blown up!" Melora cried.

Mrs. Forrest nodded. "They're dynamiting. If they can clear a path before the fire perhaps they can stop its spread. Don't worry. They won't let it cross Market."

But Melora was frightened. If only they could hurry this boat! Time seemed to be the most important element. She had to get home before the family moved out. If they left, how would she ever find them? Where would they go?

Mrs. Forrest seemed to sense her growing anxiety. "Don't rush ahead in your mind, my dear," she advised. "We can only do one thing at a time."

When they reached Fisherman's Wharf the hills cut off the fire and only the smoke pall gave evidence of its existence. They left the boat to find this part of the city much as it had always been. The little houses of the Italian folk clung to the steep sides of Telegraph Hill, the homes on Russian Hill looked peaceful and unthreatened.

Mrs. Forrest led the way down the long wharf to shore and looked about purposefully for their next conveyance. She found it in the form of a milk wagon drawn by an aging horse. The weather-beaten driver had apparently been delivering his wares as calmly as if no threat of disaster hung over the city.

Mrs. Forrest ran into the street to hail him and after a few moments of discussion she waved to Melora.

"Come along! Hurry! This man is going to get us as far as Nob Hill. He hasn't had a look at the fire yet himself, so he's willing to take a couple of passengers."

They piled into the wagon and the driver whipped up his horse. In spite of the way the air was shattered now and then by an explosion, all this part of town seemed secure, remote from danger. Only the shingles and broken glass in the street, the occasional chimney bricks gave evidence of the recent earthquake. But as their wagon bumped over cobblestones, the milk cans rattling, they began to meet more throngs of refugees pouring down cross streets carrying everything from bedding to pets. Some people pushed baby carriages and doll carriages—anything on wheels that could be loaded with possessions. Some had even managed to attach wheels to the trunks they dragged or pushed.

Now there was an ominous rain of cinders from smoke clouds overhead. Melora could hear them pattering on the roof of the wagon. There was sifting ash too, smudging their cheeks, leaving sooty streaks on their clothing. Still the horse plodded on through streets where homes stood as usual. The uncertain populace, earthquake-wary, gathered on doorsteps, or on the sidewalk, watching the refugees, calling to them for news, wondering whether to join their flight.

A dozen times men stopped their wagon, tried to bargain with the driver to turn about, take them and their goods in the opposite direction. But Mrs. Forrest's will still prevailed. Melora felt they might make faster progress by getting out and walking. Mrs. Forrest, however, shook her head.

"Wait," she said. "Not yet. There'll be walking enough before we're through."

Then, just below the crest of Nob Hill, a soldier in uniform and tightly wound puttees stopped them and commandeered the wagon, turning them out. In their place he put two old women and several younger women with babies, ordering the driver to turn and head for Golden Gate Park.

Melora was glad enough to be on foot. Now they needn't wait impatiently while the milk wagon struggled against the tide of humanity coming down the streets. The soldier made no attempt to stop them and they hurried on their way.

Nob Hill was black with thousands watching the fire, and more thousands pouring away from it. Now Melora could hear the roar and crackle. The dynamite explosions seemed frighteningly close. Through and around and intermingled with all other sound was the throbbing hum of the throngs. She had never heard anything like it before. It was like the rush of a sea, murmuring and pounding. The sound was made up of many things—of voices and the treading of feet on pavements, of the dragging of trunks and the wails of children, with now and then, strangely enough, the ripple of laughter.

The new Fairmount Hotel, still in the process of being completed, stood at the crest of the hill, its great white mass presiding serenely over lesser establishments. All about were the mansions of the wealthy, built in "bonanza" times when gold and silver lodes were making men wealthy overnight. This was not "old" San Francisco, perhaps, but it was silver-spoon San Francisco. Somehow one could not imagine such vast residences as Mrs. Leland Stanford's house, and the Mark Hopkins Institute of Art next to it, going up in flames. Melora experienced a sense of solid security in passing them on the street. While people stood at the windows of every tower that faced south, there seemed to be no undue alarm. Nob Hill was powerful and safe.

At the top of California Street Melora looked about, listening automatically for something she did not hear. For a moment she could not place the strangeness, and then she knew. The cable slots were still. For the first time since she could remember there was no clattering and chattering in those slots where the cables ran which pulled cars up and down San Francisco's hills.

Mrs. Forrest found her way to a place where she could climb upon a low wall and see the whole city toward the south. Melora clambered up beside her, thinking that Quent Seymour lived only a block or two from this spot, wondering about him for the first time. He'd written her once while she was away. A very proper letter without any reference to the little game they'd been playing. His mother had gone to New York, he said, to visit his sister Gwen until her school was out. So he and his father were rattling around in the Seymour house with nobody but a few servants for company. He'd sounded bored with his father's insurance office, where he had recently gone to work, and he wished Melora would hurry home so they could stir up some excitement around the place.

But as she followed Mrs. Forrest, inching her way along the wall, Melora forgot about Quent or where he might be at this moment. A good section of the town beyond Market showed only smouldering ruin and the smoking skeletons of burned buildings. But down near the Embarcadero along the water front, and in other sections across Market the fire burned furiously.

"The Palace is all right!" Mrs. Forrest cried in a relieved voice. "I knew it would stand!"

Melora sought out the square white building with its dozens of bay windows reflecting the light. It was true that the Palace was untouched, but all too close, flames leaped and roared. You could hear the sound of them clearly.

"I've got to get down there," Mrs. Forrest said and once more there was a tremor in her voice. "Melora, do you think—"

A man on the wall nearby heard her and spoke. "No use trying to get near the Palace, ma'am. They won't let you through the fire lines. That whole section's nothing but history now."

"But what about the Palace water supply?" Mrs. Forrest protested. "I understood—"

He shook his head. "That's been exhausted wetting down the nearest buildings. I was over there earlier. There's no hope—everyone's moved out."

Mrs. Forrest gave a long, shuddering sigh and the feather flags on her hat drooped a little with their burden of soot and cinders.

"I—I'm sorry," Melora said softly.

For a moment or two longer Mrs. Forrest stood on the wall watching the deceptively calm look of bay windows, as yet uncracked, unmelted by fire. Then she got stiffly down from the wall.

"Of course Howard is safe by now and has saved what he can. We'll get together later. For the time being I'd better stay with you, Melora."

Without further words they left the wall and started downhill.

"We'll go straight to your house now," Mrs. Forrest said. "I'll breathe easier once you're reunited with your family."

They walked quickly along, sometimes picking their way over the bricks from a fallen chimney, sometimes skirting a collapsed wall. For the most part the earthquake damage didn't seem too serious. The city would repair itself in no time, if only the fire could be stopped.

There were still moments when the earth jarred and

trembled. Then Melora and Mrs. Forrest clung to each other, their hearts pounding. But these quakes were nothing and Mrs. Forrest said they were likely to continue for months until the earth settled into its new creases.

Now, as they neared Melora's neighborhood, it was plain that some of the houses along the way had already been deserted. Other families were standing their ground, unwilling to give up until the fire was upon them. Here and there soldiers stood guard against looting, but the actual fire lines were still close to Market Street.

By the time they reached the Cranbys' block, the air was hot with the smell of burning. Every breath of wind carried stinging cinders. Constantly Melora dusted her clothes free of white ash and fine black particles.

They hurried down the block, anxiety lending speed to their steps. There was no telling how long it would be before the fire leaped across the protection of Market Street and exploded in this direction, sweeping everything before it.

Melora could see her own house now, her own front door. The sense of relief made her feel almost limp for a moment. Until now there had been an unspoken dread at the back of her mind. But little outward damage was apparent. The windows were open and she took further heart from that. Surely it meant the family was still home.

"You go up to the front door and see what's what," Mrs. Forrest said. "One of us needs to stay outside to keep an eye on the fire. If your family's gone, Melora, come right out."

Melora nodded and hurried toward the steps. A soldier crossed the street and called to her.

"Where're you going, Miss?"

She turned, hoping he wasn't going to stop her.

"This is where I live. The windows are open, so the family must still be inside."

"Doesn't mean a thing, Miss," the soldier said. "Windows are left open by orders because of the blasting. They'd all blow out otherwise and make that much more flying glass. Anyway I think everyone's out of that house."

"May I go in anyway?" Melora pleaded. "There's —there's something I want to save." If the family had left, she must make sure that the statue of Kwan Yin from her father's study had gone with them.

Evidently he'd decided that she wasn't a looter because he grinned and stepped out of her way. She waited for no more, but gathered up her heavy broadcloth skirt and ran up the steep flight of steps from the sidewalk. At the turn she looked back and saw that Mrs. Forrest was talking to the soldier and not even looking her way. She covered the remaining steps and, finding the door ajar, slipped through into the dim hall.

3

THE GOLDEN FACE OF KWAN YIN

The house was utterly quiet. The quiet of desertion. Broken glass from a hall mirror crunched under her feet. The newel post was tilted at an odd angle. She held her breath, listening, but there were only the creaking sounds of emptiness.

She picked up her skirts and ran lightly up the long flight of narrow stairs to the second floor. Here chunks of plaster were strewn across the carpet and there were footprints and smudges in the white dust where others had crossed the hall.

When she reached the third floor she ran along the dim hallway toward the closed door of the study. Did her father know by now what was happening to San Francisco, she wondered.

She flung open the study door and ran toward the little alcove her father had built to do Kwan Yin special honor, show her off to best effect. The niche stood bare and empty and for an instant she thought the statue must have been jarred to the floor in the quake. But though she looked all about she found no trace of it. Even the carved stand of teakwood that had been made especially for the statue was gone. Someone else must have remembered too and rescued it.

She stepped to the front window and looked down into the street where Mrs. Forrest still talked to the soldier. Beyond the lower rooftop of the house across the way, Melora could see the ominous thickening of smoke. It billowed upwards, pulsing with a wickedly vivid light on its underside. So close it seemed—she must hurry, hurry.

Down the stairs she ran to the second floor hall. The strip of carpet softened her steps and above her own labored breathing she heard another sound—a stealthy, slipping sound from the first floor. Breathlessly she came to a halt with one hand on the bannister at the top of the stairs. There was someone else in the house. Not the soldier or Mrs. Forrest, who would move boldly and probably call to her. Someone who tiptoed furtively, cutting off her retreat to the front door. Looter? Thief?

She slid one foot toward the top step and the whole staircase seemed to shriek with the creaking of the board. In the hall below the tiptoeing ceased. There was complete silence all through the house. But it was a waiting silence in which Melora's heart thudded wildly. As she listened the intruder drew a gasping breath.

"Who—who's there?" she quavered faintly.

There was an exclamation from the floor below. "Missy M'lory! How you come this place?"

She laughed in relief and rushed down the stairs. She could have hugged the little man in blue linen with the pigtail coiled neatly at the back of his head. Except that he was always too dignified for hugging.

"Quong Sam! Why are you here alone? Where has the family gone?"

"I stay for take care house," he told her calmly.

"Fam'ly go Lafayette Square. I tell 'um go Bonner house, but you Mama say no wantchee."

Melora well knew how her mother felt about the Bonner house, where she had lived after coming here from Virginia City. Mama had no head for finances and she had always resented the decision her mother and husband made to rent the house and move into smaller quarters. Since the move she had refused adamantly to set foot in the house, or have anything to do with the tenants. Until lately, Gran had taken care of all details concerning the house. Now that Gran no longer took an interest, Papa did what he could when he was home.

"But you can't stay here, Sam," Melora cried. "I'm with Mrs. Forrest now. Suppose you come along with us."

He closed his eyes—a familiar gesture signifying resistance—and then opened them and stared at her unblinkingly.

"Fire come, I go," he said. "Fire no come, I no go."

She shook her head in despair, knowing she could never budge his determination, once he'd made up his mind. At least she knew where to find the family now and the major portion of her anxiety was slipping away.

"All right, Sam—if you must. But take care. We need you."

"I take plenty care," he promised. "This house no burn, you see."

She started toward the door and then turned back. "Sam, did somebody take Papa's Kwan Yin away?"

This time he nodded vigorously and waved toward the parlor. "Me catchee lady god. He takee care this house fine."

Melora gave him one look and then ran past him through the parlor door. The black teakwood table from China had been pulled before the front bay window, and right in the middle of it rested the statue of Kwan Yin on her carved stand. The lovely blue coils of her hair had been unruffled by earthquake shock, her long ear lobes, bespeaking great wisdom, were unchipped, and her golden face with its benevolent and compassionate smile was turned toward the south and the fire.

Quickly Melora reached for the statue, but Quong Sam was quicker still, gently patting down her hand as he had done sometimes when she was a child reaching toward danger.

"You no touch!" he cried. "Him velly good for keep away fire. Him watchee, house no burn."

A sudden vibration shook the floor beneath their feet. Kwan Yin tilted forward and then settled back as the shock passed.

"You go outside, Missy M'lory," Quong Sam said severely, and at the same time a loud halloo reached them from the street.

Melora glanced out the window and saw the young soldier coming up the steps.

"Hey there, Miss!" he called. "You all right? Come on out of there right away! The lady here wants you."

Quong Sam fled into the dimness of the rear hall. Quite evidently he was in hiding lest he be ordered out, and the soldier had no notion of his presence in the house. Melora snatched up the statue and its stand and ran to the door, carrying them tenderly. Behind her she heard muttered imprecations from Quong Sam, but there was no way he could stop her now without betraying himself.

The soldier waited for her at the turn of the steps. Melora smiled as she ran down toward the sidewalk.

"Look—I got what I went after." She held up the Kwan Yin to show him and hurried to join Mrs. Forrest. That lady stared at the statue in disapproval.

"We can't eat that," she said. "If you were going to carry anything, why didn't you look for food?"

Food? The thought of it had never entered Melora's mind. She shifted the weight of the statue in her arms. It was fairly heavy and its shape was awkward, but she did not regret rescuing it. Her father would be pleased. There were some things more important than food.

She explained to Mrs. Forrest about Quong Sam as they went on and that the family had gone to Lafayette Square.

Mrs. Forrest nodded. "Good. We'll head toward Van Ness and then go north to California. I hope you feel like walking. Why hasn't Quong Sam skipped out to Chinatown?"

"Oh, he'd stand by us," Melora said with conviction. "We belong to him. Anyway, I don't think he has any relatives. Only a nephew he's sending to college over in Berkeley. At least that's the excuse he gives everytime he wants to disappear for a few days—that he's going to see his nephew. Mama says the nephew is a myth Sam has been using for the last twenty years. So I don't really know if he has anyone."

As they retreated along the street Melora glanced up at empty windows, wondering about people she knew. Not that she had many friends in this somewhat rundown neighborhood. Most of Mama's friends lived up on Nob Hill, or west of Van Ness.

Now, as the fire lines were pushed still farther back, a new exodus of refugees began streaming across their path up the hill. One woman fell into step beside Mrs. Forrest for a little while, carrying an empty bird cage.

"There's no more room in Union Square," the woman told them. "There're people swarming over every inch. But I wasn't staying. Looks like the fire may head that way before night."

She rushed on, the bird cage still clutched in her hands. A block farther along they came upon an old man sitting on a trunk out in the middle of the street. He was calmly strumming a banjo and singing:

When you hear dem bells go ding-ling-ling
All join 'round and sweetly sing
And when the verse am over
In the chorus all join in,
There'll be a hot time in the old town tonight. . . .

Melora had to laugh and he caught her eye and waved.

"Just waiting for a cable car," he called. Then, with a glance at the quiet slot at his feet, "Might be a long wait."

Half a block later Melora glanced back to see that he had tucked his banjo under his arm and was dragging his trunk over cobblestones, pulling it by a rope through the handle.

Now and then a flock of frightened pigeons soared above them, seeking safety, even as human beings were seeking it.

On ahead the familiar sign of the bookshop of Gower & Ellis hung at a crazy angle, where the earthquake had jarred it. The glass show window of the shop had been shattered and a young man knelt in the window, gathering up volumes which had been stacked there for display.

Melora didn't know his last name, though she'd heard Mr. Gower call him Tony, but she remembered him with interest. The last time she had been in the bookstore with Mama she'd had an odd interchange with this young man. Mama had been rather annoyed about it. Melora had known Tony by sight, since this was the Cranbys' favorite bookshop. On this occasion he had done rather a skillful job of separating her from her mother, and when Mama had entered into a discussion with Mr. Gower, he had said a most astonishing thing. Melora remembered his words very well and had thought about his behavior more than once since that day. Though without the indignation Mama thought she should feel.

The young man had told her quite frankly that he'd been wanting to talk to her ever since he'd first seen her come into the store. He liked her taste in books, he said. Henry James, for instance—there was a writer! He was glad to see she didn't read that sentimental stuff her younger sister was so fond of. Apparently he had been observing the tastes of the whole family.

That was when Mama had discovered what was happening and hurried back to sweep Melora out from under the young book clerk's interested gaze. Melora had been curious about him ever since. He didn't in the least fit the pattern of the young men she knew and it might have been fun to talk to him.

Now it didn't seem strange to come opposite the shop window and find him kneeling in it, looking straight at her over the stack of books in his arms. His skin was rather dark and he had thick dark hair and eyes that were velvety brown under heavy lashes. Italian, probably, Mama had said, and "bold like those Italians so often are."

"Good afternoon, Mrs. Forrest, Miss Cranby." Tony spoke as calmly as though he had fully expected them to turn up outside his window. "Rather a warm day for April."

Mrs. Forrest looked surprised and then laughed. "It is, indeed, and likely to be warmer. Is Mr. Gower planning to move his place of business?"

"I'm not sure," Tony said. "But it's possible that we may take a short leave of absence. For alterations. Oh, Miss Cranby—we have something for you. Something your grandmother, Mrs. Bonner, ordered. Won't you come in?"

Mrs. Forrest looked off in the direction of the fire uncertainly. "This is hardly the time—"

"Perhaps we could sit down for just a minute," Melora suggested.

At once Tony waved them into the shop and brought folding chairs. Mrs. Forrest said her feet were beginning to hurt and sat down gratefully. After all, she admitted, there was no immediate hurry and a rest would do them good.

Since electricity and gas had been turned off right after the earthquake, it was dark inside. Mr. Gower was working by the light of a single candle and Melora saw that he was packing books into a cardboard carton. He peered short-sightedly through his gold-rimmed glasses when Tony spoke to him, and came around a counter to greet them.

"Good afternoon, Miss Cranby, Mrs. Forrest," he said. "Tony is right about that order for a book. Mrs. Bonner asked us to get the red leather edition of Kingsley's *The Water-Babies* some time ago. It just came in yesterday. Hand it to her, Tony. Compliments of the house, Miss Cranby. Please give it to your grandmother." He tugged at his gray mustache with an air of vague gallantry.

Melora started to protest, but Mr. Gower waved his hands sadly. "These books are nothing but fuel now. And your grandmother has long been a valued customer. Please give it to her."

Melora took the small leather-bound volume from Tony. She remembered that Grandmother had ordered it for Alec, but reading *The Water-Babies* aloud to Alec didn't seem a very likely prospect at the moment. However, she could not refuse Mr. Gower's gesture.

A sharp command was barked at them suddenly from the doorway and Melora turned to see a soldier standing there.

"Hey, get that light out!" he shouted. "The mayor

has ordered no lights. We've got fires enough to worry about."

Mr. Gower puffed out the candle and the blustery soldier disappeared.

Somewhat rested, Mrs. Forrest was ready to go on again. As Tony walked with them to the door, he noted the statue Melora carried.

"I see you set value on important things," he said. "Kwan Yin and *The Water-Babies*. Items worth saving in a fire."

"I'm not so sure about that," said Mrs. Forrest tartly. "Come along, Melora—we've still a lot of walking ahead of us."

She went out the door, but Tony spoke again before Melora could follow her. "Where are you going now, Melora Cranby?"

She paused in the doorway. "Our Chinese cook says the family has taken refuge in Lafayette Square. We'll look for them there."

"But doesn't your grandmother own a big house out that way?"

"Yes, on Washington Street, across from the square. I expect we'll go there eventually, though tenants are occupying it." She was aware of Mrs. Forrest waiting for her outside the door, but she stayed a moment longer. "Where do you live?" she asked him.

"Near the top of Russian Hill," Tony said. "Though my mother's family is on Telegraph Hill. We should be all right."

"I do hope so," Melora said. "Thank you for thinking of the book. I'd better go now—Mrs. Forrest is waiting for me."

"It wasn't the book alone I was thinking of," he said softly. "I'll see you again, Melora."

She rejoined Mrs. Forrest in some confusion. This young man left her with a pleasant sense of exhilaration. Knowing him better might be interesting. When *would* she see him again?

As she walked on at Mrs. Forrest's side, carrying Kwan Yin and the book, she found herself plagued by a desire to look back at the Gower & Ellis shop. She didn't give in to the urge until she was a good block away. Then she glanced over her shoulder. Tony knelt in the window again. He wasn't working at his task but staring after her with the frankest interest. When he saw her head turn he waved to her and she smiled and waved back.

Mrs. Forrest glanced at her appraisingly. "That's a bright young man—Tony Ellis—and I think he'll climb, if I know his type. I can't see him hidden forever in a bookshop. He's too flamboyant. I suspect he likes an audience—that one."

"Ellis?" Melora repeated in surprise. "You mean of Gower & Ellis? But I thought—that is, Mama said he was probably Italian."

"His father was John Ellis, Mr. Gower's partner. He died some years ago. I suppose Tony will own half the store one of these days—if there's any store left to own. So Mr. Gower must be trying to break him in. But he's Italian enough on his mother's side. That's what gives him the exotic touch. Quite a collection there—opera singers, restaurant owners, fishermen. Odd sort of marriage for his mother, with books on the other side. I wonder which branch Tony takes after. Come along, my dear, you're lagging a little."

Melora hurried her steps, but her thoughts were on Tony's background. It all sounded different and fascinating. So different from Quent, whose father was in insurance—a dull sort of business, as even Quent himself admitted—and whose mother was very "old" San Francisco.

Even in Chicago life had been enough different to make it great fun to set things down in her diary. She'd always loved to turn happenings into words. But at home there had often been days on end when nothing seemed worth recording. The sudden realization came to her that since this morning the whole face of existence had changed for all of them. She would hardly need to worry about the monotony of life for quite a while. Already there were a hundred things to write in her diary when she had it in her hands again. And one of them would be this odd meeting with Tony Ellis.

Before they reached Van Ness they had one other encounter. A grocery store keeper gestured at them from his doorway.

"Come along and help yourselves!" he invited. "It'll all burn anyway. Pick up what you can carry. Hurry, hurry!"

Along with others in the street, they dashed across and into the store. Burdened with book and statue, Melora couldn't manage many tins or packages, but she juggled four or five articles into her arms. A tin of peaches, a loaf of bread—the last in the shop—a tin of tomatoes, and one of string beans. All sensible things which she was sure Mrs. Forrest would approve. Then one little exotic item she couldn't resist—a small tin of caviar. She'd tasted it once at a luncheon at the Palace Hotel and had loved the strange, salty flavor. But she hid it under the other things, knowing caviar wasn't the best possible fare for refugees.

Mrs. Forrest hesitated no more than a moment. Then she pulled up her street skirt, loosened the waistband of her top underskirt and swished herself out of it. Into the voluminous skirt she piled as much foodstuff as she could carry, tied the skirt openings in knots and slung the improvised bag over her shoulder.

Melora bit her lips to keep from smiling. Mrs. Forrest, still wearing her big hat with the increasingly bedraggled feathers, and carrying the huge skirt-bag over her shoulder, made a strange picture indeed.

More and more now along the street they came upon pitiful heaps of belongings, either moved out of the houses and then abandoned when the occupants left, or dropped by the way because they grew too heavy to carry. Never, never, Melora thought, would she let Kwan Yin join their sad company.

Van Ness was a wide and dignified residential avenue of fine houses. Like Market Street, it might make a fire break if one was necessary. Considerable earthquake damage was evident in the buckled pavement, roof tiles cluttering the street and fences twisted awry.

They began to climb toward Lafayette Square, but as they came in sight of sloping, grassy banks and high walks, a new anxiety filled Melora. The square—it was a park really, covering several blocks—was black with people. There must be thousands up here—and how could she ever find her family in such a throng?

Children and dogs and cats were all intermingled. Here and there some lucky family had set up a tent for shelter against the coming chill of evening and the dampness that was inevitable.

Mrs. Forrest stopped helplessly at the foot of cement steps leading up through a corner of the square. She too seemed to find the crowd greater than she had expected. But as they stood there, looking upward, a sudden shout came from a grassy summit above and a small figure catapulted out from the crowd and tore down the steps toward them. It was Alec and he flung himself upon Melora, so that she had to pull Kwan Yin hastily out of his way. Book and tinned goods she dropped for the moment so that she could circle Alec's small body with one free arm. He was pudgy with sweaters, and one long black stocking was slipping from its garter.

He nuzzled his blond head into her shoulder like a young butting goat, expressing his delight boy-fashion.

"Grandmother *said* you'd find us!" he cried. "She

said Mrs. Forrest would come across somehow and Sam would tell you where to find us. Cora thinks you'd stay in Oakland and Mama is sure you've been burned to a crisp. But Gran knew."

"As you can see, young man," Mrs. Forrest broke in, "we are sooty but unsinged. Now suppose you stop choking your sister and lead the way to your camp. My feet are killing me and this load is heavy."

4

REFUGEES

An umbrella had been set up as partial protection from cinders and char, as well as from the wind, and Adelina Cranby lay upon a blanket with her head and shoulders under the umbrella. She did not move as Melora and Mrs. Forrest wound their way toward her between other "camps," stepping over outstretched legs and around strange assortments of possessions.

Melora saw that her mother's cheeks were white, instead of their usual rosy tint, and there was a streaking of tears in the soot smears on her face. To find her neat little mother with a dirty face was almost as startling as finding the city on fire. Mrs. Cranby's sunny pile of hair was hidden now beneath a gray veil tied under her chin, and she wore a long coat over shirtwaist and skirt. On the grass beside her sat Cora in similar dress, looking pretty in spite of disaster. She held a small green bottle of smelling salts and was regarding her mother anxiously. Grandmother Bonner was nowhere in sight.

Alec left Melora's side and ran ahead to drop on the grass beside his mother. "Mama, Melora's here! She hasn't gone and got burned up at all!"

Cora turned with a cry that was part laughter and part tears. What a pretty thing she was, Melora thought, as she often did when looking at Cora. Her hair, fluffing out from beneath the veil, was even fairer than Mama's and her eyes were as blue.

"Mama's had such an awful time," Cora said. "She didn't want to leave the house at all, but Gran said there was no point in staying till the last minute."

Her mother held out a smooth, plump hand to Melora, who knelt to take it in her own larger one.

"I'm so glad you're here!" Mrs. Cranby cried. "How you ever found us, I can't think. You were another worry on top of leaving the house and having to give up everything your Papa and I have lived with and loved for so many years. Everything we've built together!"

Tears showed signs of starting again, and Mrs. Forrest spoke quickly. "You're not the only one, Addy. Thousands of other people are losing everything too."

Mama dabbed at her eyes with a scrap of lace handkerchief. "You don't understand, Nell. You never did have an ounce of sentiment in you. It's our life that's going up in flames—Andrew's and mine."

"Nonsense!" said Mrs. Forrest. "Your lives haven't been touched at all."

But Melora squeezed her mother's hand sympathetically. Mama wasn't so awfully strong, and she'd always lived a gay, happy, comfortable life. This would be harder for her than for a woman like Mrs. Forrest.

"Don't you worry," Melora said. "We stopped in at the house an hour or so ago and it's still all right. Quong Sam's there and you know he'll take care of everything if it's possible. Look, I've brought out Papa's Kwan Yin."

Her mother's gaze rested briefly on the golden face of the statue and then she closed her eyes.

"Ugh—that thing! I don't see why you had to pick that to rescue."

"Papa is fond of it," Melora reminded her. She and

Cora exchanged a secret smile. It was something of a joke in the family the way Mama was jealous of Kwan Yin. She had never liked the fact that Papa felt he should have a retreat at the top of the house, where he could close the door and be quiet with his own thoughts. Mama said he was home so seldom that she wanted him near her every minute. Since his study was Kwan Yin's haven, she had centered a certain resentment on the goddess.

Mrs. Forrest had seated herself on the grass and taken off her high laced shoes. Now she was sorting over the items she had obtained from the grocery shop, while Alec helped her eagerly.

"Where is Gran?" Melora asked her sister.

Cora gestured uphill. "She said she'd climb to higher ground and see what the fire was doing."

"How is she?" Melora went on. "I was worried about her before I left for Chicago."

"You go see for yourself," Cora told her. "She's surprised us all. I'd never have thought it!"

Melora set the statue carefully out of harm's way beneath the umbrella and got to her feet. The book she kept with her. She would indeed go see for herself. Both Quong Sam's and Alec's remarks made it sound as though Grandmother had taken full charge as she used to do. Mama had never been the managing kind except when it came to matters of etiquette and propriety.

Melora climbed the hill between groups which had encamped in the square. Some people looked stunned, as if they couldn't believe what was happening, could only sit apathetically, staring at nothing. But mostly everyone seemed to be behaving as if this were a picnic, an adventure. They lounged about in curious costumes with odd possessions gathered nearby, and laughed and joked as if this were a great lark. There was none of the panic here that Melora had seen on the Oakland mole. The most frightened ones had already run away. She smiled readily at strangers, who as readily smiled back, and she liked the feeling of comradeship that seemed to draw these hundreds of refugees together.

She found her grandmother standing with her back against the peeling trunk of a eucalyptus tree, her gaze fixed on the city below. She had not tied a veil over her head and she wore no hat, so that there were bits of black char in the silver gray of her hair. Yet she managed somehow to look as neat and tidy as usual, and there was a serenity about her, even as she watched the burning city.

Tears closed Melora's throat. Until this moment she had felt that she must keep putting out energy, that she must not give up, that she must struggle toward this reuniting with her family. But now a reaction of weakness swept through her.

"Gran!" she cried and stumbled blindly up the last rise of hill.

Grandmother Melora Bonner turned and the warmth of her smile was like an embrace, even before she held out her arms.

"I knew you'd find us if your train came through," Grandmother said.

Melora put her wet cheek against her grandmother's softly crumpled one and held tight.

"All the way home I've longed for San Francisco!" she cried. "And now there'll be no San Francisco. It's going—all of it!"

"Stop that this minute!" said her grandmother, holding her away. "What nonsense are you talking? Do you think any fire on earth can burn down the important things that make up a town like this one?"

A crash of musical chords startled Melora and she looked over her grandmother's shoulder at the strangest of sights. There on a level stretch of ground a piano had been somehow hauled. And sitting on an upended wooden box before it was a thin young man banging away at the keys. His family leaned on the piano, or stood about him, raising their voices enthusiastically in song.

"That's what I mean," Gran said. "You can't down spirit like that."

But Melora did not look at the singers as she choked back her emotion. She looked at the fragile figure of her grandmother, standing there so bravely.

Gran stirred at her side. "The fire is still south of Market, but I suspect that it will reach our house during the night."

"Don't you think we ought to go to the Bonner place?" Melora asked. "Is Mama still—"

"She is indeed," Gran said. "She's full of her silly notion about refusing to beg from our tenants, the Hoopers. But give her a night in the open and I think she'll be more sensible. It won't hurt us all to camp out for one night. Well, let's go open some cans of beans. We carried all the foodstuff we could in a pillowcase and it looks as though we might be eating a right smart number of beans in the next few days."

"You can have the beans," said Melora. "I'm going to have a caviar sandwich." For the first time she remembered the book in her hands and held it out. "Gran, Mr. Gower sent you this from his bookshop with his compliments."

Grandmother took the small red volume with an air of satisfaction. "How thoughtful of him. I've been wanting this to read to Alec. It will come in handy now."

And strangely enough it did. When they'd managed to make a cold meal out of tins they huddled around Gran, two to a blanket. And in the fading light of an evening that would never grow completely dark, she read sweetly aloud from *The Water-Babies*.

Melora listened, carried back to the day when she and Cora had been as young as Alec, and they too had listened raptly to the story of Tom, the little chimney sweep who was given the magical power to live under water. She remembered the chiming and tinkling of the river—so tempting to the dirty little sweep. She felt like the sweep herself now, with grime on her face and hands, and no water for washing.

When it grew too dark to read the words, Grandmother closed the book. But her voice went on, strong as the river itself:

> "Clear and cool, clear and cool,
>   By laughing shallow, and dreaming pool;
>   Cool and clear, cool and clear,
> By shining shingle, and foaming weir;
> Under the crag where the ouzel sings,
> And the ivied wall where the church-bell rings,
>   Undefiled, for the undefiled;
> Play by me, bathe in me, mother and child."

Several children from other groups had crawled nearer to listen, and there was a quiet creeping away when Gran's voice stopped.

Mrs. Forrest talked quietly to Grandmother for a while, wondering about her son and how she might get in touch with him. But all that would have to wait till tomorrow. Mama fell into a restless sleep, with Alec beside her, while Melora sat with her arm linked in Cora's listening to the frightening sounds of the red, angry night.

The fire was much worse after dark. Flames lit up the billowing clouds of smoke overhead, painting them savagely with crimson and orange and pale yellow. The fire had shot in a dozen new directions and there was a pulsing of heat in the air. At least no one was very cold.

To while away the long hours when sleep would not come, Melora told her sister about Chicago and their cousin's wedding. And about the trip home and the struggle she and Mrs. Forrest had had to get across to San Francisco in the early afternoon.

Once Cora asked about Quent. "Do you know what's happened to him?"

Melora shook her head. She had hardly thought of Quent since that moment on Nob Hill when they had been a block or two from his home.

"How dreadful for you not to know," Cora whispered. "But I'm sure he's all right."

For an instant Melora was tempted to confide the truth about her make-believe engagement, but she suppressed the impulse. Cora was the bubbling-over sort who could never keep such news to herself and this was not the time to upset Mama still further. Besides, all that seemed remote and unimportant now.

"I'm sure the Seymour place will escape, way at the top of the hill," Cora comforted.

Melora said nothing. Hilltops could burn too. Nob Hill and Telegraph Hill, and even high Russian Hill, where Tony Ellis lived. She closed her eyes and thought about her meeting with him that afternoon.

She could remember him quite clearly as he'd watched her with that bright, laughing look when she turned to glance over her shoulder. He had said quite distinctly that it had not been the book alone he was thinking of when he'd invited her into the shop. He'd behaved as though she were someone special whom he wanted to know. And he'd said he would see her again. These were things to think about pleasantly now. They were thoughts to hold off thoughts of the fire.

What was happening to Tony now? *Would* she see him again?

Far to the north the sky was a clear dark blue and the stars still shone. It was comforting to know that somewhere there were clear skies and shining stars. Perhaps Tony too was looking at them.

5

THE
BONNER HOUSE

The refugees in Lafayette Square talked and sang and dozed and woke through all that night of flame and shadow. In the morning a blood-red sun looked down at them briefly with its single eye, before vanishing behind the smoke pall. Morning light was pale and tired and as people stood up all over the park to stretch cramped limbs and shake out rumpled clothing, it became evident that the fire had not abated. It was creeping about below Nob Hill now.

Apparently not even the mansions of the great were to be spared. But still it had not crossed Van Ness, and Lafayette Square remained a haven.

Newcomers to the park said the Palace Hotel had burned late yesterday afternoon, and told how flames had poured from every bay window. Mrs. Forrest went off by herself for a little while. When she came back her eyes were red and it was Mama's turn to do some comforting.

Most of the buildings of the business section had gone during the night, and the fire had closed in on Portsmouth Square. Dew fell toward dawn and clothes were damp, but the morning was warm again, because of the unusual summery weather and the heat generated by the fire.

Melora, waking from an uneasy doze, shook the leaves of a nearby bush free of water drops and dampened her handkerchief in a sketchy effort to scrub her face and hands clean. Quong Sam had filled some bottles with water from the boiler in the cellar at home before the family left, but this of course must be saved for drinking.

"Are we going to stay right here all day?" Alec asked when they had breakfasted on beans again and had a few sips of the carefully rationed water.

Mama had recovered to some extent and was sitting up to comb her long fair hair, before she bound it up and tied the veil over it again. She was coughing now and then and Gran looked at her in concern.

"I don't like the sound of that cough," she said firmly. "It's time to forget your notion that if you are not mistress of the Bonner house you won't set foot in it."

Mama, coughing again, offered no further objections and Gran looked at Melora.

"Do you think you could walk over to Washington and see if the Hoopers have any room for us? Or at least for your mother."

Melora was glad of a chance to move about and so was Alec. He jumped up quickly.

"May I go with Melora, Mama? I want to see what's happening."

"I suppose you may," his mother said doubtfully. "But, Melora, don't let him out of your sight for a minute. You know how he is."

As they started out together, Melora glanced fondly at the excited boy. He was tall for his eight years and held himself erectly. His fine blond hair made a childish duck's tail point at the nape of his neck, but his straight mouth curved neither up nor down, and his chin was determined.

The square was so crowded that they had to worm their way across it, stepping over reclining figures, detouring around individual camps. Now and then they saw someone they knew, but for the most part Mama's friends had not taken refuge in the park. Probably they were still on Nob Hill, or safe in their homes farther west. Alec, however, had found some boys from his school and one of them had a tent.

"I wish we didn't have to go to any old house," he said. "Why couldn't we have a tent and just stay in the square? Maybe the Bonner house will burn down too, so what's the use of going into it? Melora, are you scared?"

She considered a moment before she shook her head. "Not any more. I was frightened all the way across the bay and right up to the minute when I found you were all gone from our house. Then I think I stopped being frightened and got used to the whole thing."

But she knew that her brave words weren't wholly true. You could never get used to a sight like this. You just didn't think about it all the time.

"How about you?" she asked Alec.

He danced a little on the path beside her. "It's an adventure, Melora. Just like in a story book. And I'm not scared any more. It was only when the house started shaking and I heard that awful roaring sound like express trains running underground that I was scared."

He told her how he had been thrown out of bed to find the floor rolling like waves at sea, and things crashing all through the house. He had run into his mother's room and in the early morning light he had found her trying to steady herself against the wall. Cora came in too and they all clung to each other. It had seemed like forever before it stopped, though he guessed it was less than a minute.

"What about Gran?" Melora asked.

"It's funny about Gran," Alec puzzled. "Day before yesterday she stayed in bed and wouldn't get up at all. Mama and Quong Sam were real worried about her. Mama said it was just like she had stopped being interested in living. She's been getting more and more like that lately. She didn't even get out of bed during the earthquake. But then, after the shaking stopped, Mama just slid down the wall in a faint. Quong Sam came rushing upstairs and said we'd better all get outside—but there was Mama on the floor and he went across the hall to get Gran. I could hear him sort of scolding her the way he does. He was saying, 'You boss Missy now, you boss Missy!'

"When he brought her in, Gran was leaning on him and looking as if she didn't know just what was happening until she saw Mama on the floor, all white and still. That was when I was most scared, Melora, and I guess I started to cry. But Gran seemed to wake up and she just gave me a look. Then she said, 'Well, I suppose somebody's got to do it,' and she's been the boss Missy ever since. Melora, what about Papa?"

The crowd had grown so thick in the square that they cut down toward Gough Street where it met Washington. Melora squeezed Alec's hand.

"We'll have to find a way to let him know we're all right. He'll be terribly worried, of course. But there isn't anything we can do now."

Streaming west along Washington was the familiar rivers of wagons and carts, a sprinkling of automobiles and hundreds of refugees. But now Melora noted the great number of Chinese. So Chinatown too had burned during the night.

They fell in with the throngs on the sidewalk, but no one looked at them or paid any attention. Today the refugees were more dazed and weary than they had been the day before. All they could manage was to put one foot in front of the other and struggle along under the burden of goods they had piled on their backs or all manner of conveyance—anything that could be carried or dragged.

Before they reached the Bonner house, Alec found something to distract him from all thoughts of house or fire. The whining sound of some small creature in pain made him look down to see that a small gray-brown mongrel was cringing near the wall along the edge of the park, trying to keep from under the feet of those who passed him so heedlessly.

"Look, Melora, it's a little hurt dog!" Alec cried and knelt beside the forlorn animal.

"Be careful," Melora warned. "If he's in pain he may bite."

But Alec had a way with animals and the dog permitted himself to be examined, even licking Alec's hands.

"Melora, he's been near the fire," Alec said. "See how the fur on his back is all singed. And that's a bad burn on his hind leg. Come, fellow, I'll take care of you."

Melora made no objection. The dog's soft brown eyes looked lost and melancholy. He too was a refugee. Alec picked him up gently and the dog's wet pink tongue licked his ear.

As they started across the street, they were surprised to discover Quong Sam sound asleep behind the railing of the front balcony. His head and shoulders showed between the fretwork and a carpetbag with plump and bulging sides rested below him on the top step.

Alec rushed up the steps, the dog in his arms.

"Sam!" he cried, as though the circumstances under which they met were perfectly usual. "Wake up! I've found a dog with a sore leg. Can you fix him, Sam?"

Quong Sam unbent and stood up, a Cranby blanket about his shoulders, and his pigtail hanging outside. "I fix-um dog," he said calmly. "You gotchee key, Missy M'lory? We go inside."

Melora made herself ask the question, much as she feared the answer. "What's happened to our house, Sam?"

Quong Sam looked down at her, his round yellow face with its hundred pockmarks expressing the utmost in reproach. "You takee lady god—house burn. I come here."

Until this moment there had been a faint hope at the back of Melora's mind that somehow, somehow their house might have been spared. With Sam's words, the last hope crumbled.

"What about the tenants here?" she asked.

"All gone, Miss M'lory. All too much aflaid. We live this house now. More ploper house. You gotchee key?"

"I don't have a key," Melora said, "and I'm not sure —" but Sam gave her no chance to finish.

Without hesitation he stepped onto the rail of the balcony below the front bay window. The glass had broken in the quake and it took him only a moment to climb inside and nod at her solemnly through the window.

"Aw light, Missy M'lory. Now can go tell fam'ly come this house. You hully up bling 'um here."

She had to smile at his prompt solution, but she stood for a moment gazing at the three impressive stories of the house; in the rear where there was a hill they became four. This wasn't as grand a house as those on Nob Hill, but it had always seemed imposing to her eyes with its high tower looking toward the bay, its upper balconies and turrets, its windows set at odd angles. While her mother would never set foot in the house after it had been rented, she had sometimes brought her children here to walk slowly past on the other side of the street.

"Remember that your grandfather built this house, and that you were born here," she would say. "This is where we belong. If your grandfather hadn't lost all his money we might still be living here."

But even as a little girl, Melora had noted that her mother never said these things in front of Papa. Papa was great on living within one's income and he didn't feel that his salary as captain of a merchant vessel justified the occupation of a mansion. Of course Melora had come to the house now and then with Gran, but that was something they didn't mention to Mama.

Alec nudged her out of her revery. "You'd better do what Sam says. Maybe it would be fun to move into this house after all."

"We'll go find out," Melora said. "Suppose you give that dog to Sam and come back with me. You'll be needed to help move camp."

Sam had gone around to the front door and unlocked it with a great rattling of bolts. Now he beamed at them from the doorway.

"I take sma' fella," he said, reaching for the dog which Alec gave him. "You come back chop-chop and I fin' plenty chow." He started to turn away and then looked back at Melora.

"Las' night befo' fire come, Mista Kint come down for look-see fam'ly. For look-see you. I tellee you come here."

"Mista Kint" was Sam's name for Quentin Seymour.

"Then the Seymours' place is still all right?" Melora asked.

"Maybe-so for now," said Sam cautiously and waved them on their way again.

They hurried back to the camp in Lafayette Square and found the others waiting anxiously for their re-

turn. Melora gave her news, good and bad. Sam said
the Cranby house had burned. However the tenants at
the Bonner place had moved out for the moment at
least, and he thought everyone should come down
there.

Grandmother listened quietly, but Mama gave a little
moan of despair. "We've lost everything we own!
We've nothing to start life with again except the
clothes on our backs. And the Bonner house will
probably burn too!"

Cora soothed and murmured, and Mrs. Forrest, who
had recovered somewhat from the knowledge of her
own loss, snorted impatiently. But Gran regarded her
daughter without emotion.

"This isn't the first time I've started life with nothing. There wasn't much left when the Yankees burned
our place back home, either. But we did all right. And
so will you. Now stop that sniffling. We've got to move
down to the old house."

Mama opened her eyes and stared at Gran in amaze-
ment. It was many a year since she had been spoken to
as a child and she seemed more startled than angry.
After that she struggled to her feet and tried to help
as the little camp gathered its possessions together. But
she was plainly tired and the cough wracked her so
that Melora led her to a place where the blankets had
been piled.

"You stay here till we're ready to go," she whispered. "We can take care of everything."

Alec distracted his mother with an account of the
dog he had adopted. He could keep the dog, couldn't
he, he pleaded. His mother sniffed at her smelling salts
and smiled faintly. No one could begrudge Alec the
little dog at a time like this.

They hardly glanced in the direction of the billowing smoke clouds as they packed up food and blankets
and the few extra clothes brought from the Cranby

house. Now and then somebody checked just to make sure the fire's course hadn't flared suddenly in this direction.

Melora noticed Mrs. Forrest still in her feathered hat, standing on the grass in bare feet, her black lisle stockings hung over her arm and the shoes that were too tight for her swollen feet in her hand. She was reading a notice of some kind and Melora glanced at it.

"Proclamation from the Mayor," Mrs. Forrest said. "It seems that automobiles went through town yesterday giving these out."

The proclamation minced no words. Looters would be shot, it warned. No fires were to be lighted in stoves or chimneys inside any house. Citizens were to remain at home after nine o'clock at night and stay off the streets.

Mrs. Forrest passed the paper on to another group nearby and nodded at Melora. "Wise orders, I'm sure. Are we ready to go now? I haven't walked around shoeless in years, but I must say the grass feels good under my feet."

They started back shortly, straggling along with their various loads. Mama walked between Cora and Alec, leaning now and then on Alec's strong young shoulder. Melora followed carrying the Kwan Yin, the carved stand and whatever else she could manage.

At the Bonner house they found that Quong Sam had been busy in a practical way. He had gathered up fallen bricks from the chimney and built himself a little stove against the curb in the street. The water boiler in the cellar had supplied him with that precious commodity and a pan of water was heating for tea, while another pan held canned soup. The thought of hot food was enough to revive the spirits. They all dumped their possessions on the front lawn and sat down on the steps to eat.

The Hoopers had left most of their kitchen things behind and Sam was able to bring out bowls and cups and a teapot. All up and down the street those who had not fled were building little kitchens and the separate groups waved to one another cheerfully.

The vegetable soup was hot and strengthening and the sugared tea seemed a luxury. The dog lay at Alec's feet and watched him, only turning now and then to nose at the leg Quong Sam had bandaged.

"I'm going to call him Smokey," Alec said. "He's a sort of smoke color and he smells like smoke. And besides, he came out of the fire."

Sam had unearthed an old pair of carpet slippers for Mrs. Forrest and she sat with her feet hidden and tried to keep up her spirits with talk.

"Smokey doesn't look like much of a dog," she said to Alec. "But I expect that's the best kind to have. I don't think there'll be any reward offered for him, and if he decides to love you, he'll be loyal. No, thanks, Sam—no more soup."

Having finished, Gran would have braced herself to rise and go inside, but Quong Sam waved her down at once.

"You no through," he protested. "You stay here."

So they stayed where they were, while Sam vanished through the front door. Melora was watching from her place near the top of the steps when he came out on the porch again and she saw that he carried a large tray, borrowed from the tenants. But the half dozen gold and black lacquer finger bowls, each containing a scant inch of water, were plainly the treasured property of the Cranbys. Three years ago Papa had brought those bowls home from China.

Sam passed them around triumphantly—first to Gran, whom he was now accepting as head of the family. Then to Alec, as the only male present, and finally to the other four women. Mama sat up and stared bright-eyed at the lacquer bowls.

"This is very fine, Sam," Grandmother approved, "but where did you get the water? We mustn't waste any we can drink, you know."

"No dlinkee this," said Sam, bobbing his head at Gran in a quick little bow. "All over house plenty flowas. No good for flowas dlink water now. I pour off. You finish, you no thlow 'way."

When Melora received her bowl she found that Sam had added a tiny Chinese water flower, with its pale pink and green petals floating on the surface. Sam had always produced those flowers for special occasions. They looked like bits of straw until you dropped them in water, and then the leaves and petals unfolded into perfect blossoms. So, she thought, Sam's well-stuffed carpetbag had not contained his own possessions alone. What else had he brought away from the house when he had left? But it would do no good to ask. Sam loved mystery and he would divulge what he pleased in his own good time.

When they were through with their finger bowl baths —they all practically bathed in them—Sam carefully poured the water back into a flower vase to be preserved for further washing purposes. Goodness knows when they would have a full supply of water again.

"Now then," said Grandmother, taking charge again briskly, "suppose we move into the house and get settled. We need to be doing something and I think the best thing is to behave as if we planned to stay right here indefinitely."

Mama shivered and looked up at the place where bricks had fallen from the side chimney. "But what if there's another bad quake? Do you think we'll be safe inside?"

"The first quake didn't kill us and probably the next one won't either. But you can stay outside if you want to. I'm going in and look for a good bed and a nap. None of us did much sleeping last night."

Mrs. Forrest followed her up the steps, the carpet slippers slapping on her feet. "An excellent idea. And at least I don't think we need to worry about the fire. If we're in any danger the troopers will come through to let us know. There's still law and order in this town."

Alec inched his way ahead of the others, curious and eager, carrying Smokey, while Melora came up the steps last. She had always loved to come to this house whenever Gran would bring her. But how strange to be coming here now!

The massive front door was set in an archway and opened into a dim, wide hall, paneled in dark wood. The only light from outside shone through a high stained glass window on the left. A wide stairway of rich cherry wood jogged upward in the middle of the hall and a balcony rimmed the open stair well on the floor above. Downstairs, toward the front of the house, were the closed doors of the drawing room, and at the rear, facing the bay, was a smaller parlor.

Melora looked for her grandmother and saw her standing straight and proud at the foot of the stairs, playing hostess as gracefully as she must have done so often in the years that were gone. Her eyes, which had seemed lusterless for the last few months, were bright now. She blinked several times rapidly. This house must seem a lonely place to her, Melora thought. It was not Mama but Gran whose memories were most concerned with painful loss in this house. But Gran showed her feelings for no more than a moment.

"Do come upstairs and settle into your room," Gran said to Mrs. Forrest. "Of course you must stay with us until you get in touch with Howard."

Mrs. Forrest bowed graciously and went up the stairs. Gran rustled on ahead in her full black skirt, stepping casually over earthquake wreckage, and began to identify each room.

Adelina, of course, must move into the master bedroom, while Alec could have the smaller room adjoining. The guest room at the front of the house would, she was sure, be most comfortable for Mrs. Forrest. She herself preferred the small tower room which had once been her own little sitting room. As for the girls—

"There are more rooms on the third floor. May we look up there?" Melora said quickly. She too had taken to the idea of a room in a tower and she knew there was another one just above Gran's.

Her grandmother nodded her permission and went flitting from room to room among wreckage and the muss and confusion left behind by a family in flight. All these beds must be changed, of course, and the moment the girls had picked their own rooms they could come down and help. Fortunately, most of the furniture in the house belonged to her.

"We will not touch the Hoopers' clothes or best china," Gran said, "and we'll repay them for any food we eat. I don't think they'll begrudge us the use of the rest until we can purchase new supplies of our own."

Cora, running upstairs after Melora, laughed softly.

"Listen to her! She sounds as though there was no fire eating up the town a few blocks away, and as though all we had to do was run downtown to the White House and order new bedding. Yet day before yesterday she wouldn't even get up."

"Now she knows how much we need her," Melora said.

A crystal chandelier, surprisingly unhurt, hung down into the stair well from the second floor ceiling, and the balcony wound around above it. On one newel post was set a tall brass torch ending in a globe for a gas jet, broken now. Since the house was wired for electricity this was no longer used. The second floor balcony hall was paneled completely in a dark wood that reflected no light, and the girls had to grope their way to a narrower staircase leading to the third floor.

The tenants had apparently not occupied this upper floor. When Melora opened the door of the tower room the musty smell of long disuse came to her, but even dead air untainted by smoke was a relief to breathe. It did not take long, however, for the smoke smell to invade even this retreat. She flung open one of the tower windows, hoping for a clear breath from the bay, but the air was hot and dead and smoke-heavy.

Cora ran down the hall to the front of the house to find a place for herself, while Melora looked about the little room. A narrow bed stood unmade in the corner and there were a few other furnishings. She set the statue of Kwan Yin carefully upon a shelf along the wall and then turned to look at herself in the square mirror over the bureau. Streaks of soot blackened her forehead and one cheek, and she was thoroughly dusty and bedraggled. She had dampened her handkerchief again in the fingerbowl of water and now she dabbed at her face once more. Oh, for the luxury of soap and water!

Cora came in and pulled her to the window where they could look out toward the calm waters of the bay. The hills around the Golden Gate rose serene and undisturbed as always, and far out there the sky was blue and unsmirched. Only the unusual activity on the water betrayed that something was afoot in the city of San Francisco. That portion of the bay which they could glimpse was dotted with craft—everything from larger vessels to the tiniest of tugs, all well loaded with people. More refugees being taken away? Or sightseers come to stare at a city's death agonies?

"Do you think this house will burn too?" Cora

asked uneasily. "Is there any use in our trying to settle down?"

Melora shook her head. "I don't know. And Gran doesn't either. But she's smart to keep us busy. Then we won't start counting our losses. It's better not to think of those things now. Let's go down and help her."

But Cora did not move toward the door at once. Her hair, usually caught back by a hair bow at the nape of her neck, had come loose. It curled in soft tendrils about her shoulders, making her look less than her sixteen years.

"We'll pull through somehow," Melora said. "Just think of all the other times San Francisco has burned down."

Cora nodded. "I know. It isn't that. I really don't think any of this is very bad right now. There's still the feeling of excitement to key us up. But I can't *believe* in it, Melora. I keep thinking of your old rag doll, Cindy, that you used to play with as a little girl. I brought her down from the attic the other day just for a joke and put her in the chair beside your bed to greet you when you came home. And she's still sitting there. I know it!"

Melora knew what her sister meant. She'd felt that too. The Cranby house and everything in it was completely alive and clear in her mind. She could walk through it in her thoughts just as she had done yesterday afternoon in reality. She could feel the banister beneath her hand, hear the creak of that top step, see her own room—just as Mama had redone it for last Christmas. She could count all the little belongings she had not bothered to take with her on her trip to Chicago. Everything was there. Nothing was changed.

And yet it was. So dreadfully.

"Let's go down," she repeated and she and Cora turned toward the stairs together.

"I'm glad you're here, Melora," Cora said. "We've missed you."

As they reached the second floor, Quong Sam came hurrying to find them.

"Missy M'lory!" he cried. "You hully up flont door. Mista Kint here. Mista Kint in devil wagon."

Melora saw the open sympathy in her sister's eyes and could hardly suppress her irritation. She would be happy to see Quent, of course, but not in the way Cora expected.

6

BREATH OF ROSES

The "devil wagon" Melora recognized at once as Mr. Will Seymour's Oldsmobile car. "Uncle Will" they all called him by way of courtesy, though of course Quent's father wasn't a real uncle. But now it was Quent, not Uncle Will, who sat behind the wheel of the car.

He waved at the two girls as if he were on his way to a picnic. "We made it! And without another flat tire." He leaned over to speak to someone who was examining the spoked wheels on the far side of the car. "Everything all right, you think?"

There was a mumbled reply and Quent got out to see for himself.

In the tonneau sat a plump lady, middle-aged, but strikingly handsome and rather foreign-looking. She was hatless and had ignored the stylish pompadour hairdress of the day to pull glossy black wings down from a center part ending in a coil on the back of her neck. Her lips were as red as though she might have touched them with pigment, and her dark eyes had a lively snap to them. When she spoke, greeting Melora with easy friendliness, she made quick, expressive gestures with hands that were small for her size.

Heaped about her in the car were rolled-up cylinders

of various lengths and on the leather seat beside her was a huge laundry basket filled to the brim and covered over with a flowered challis wrapper.

"Good morning," Melora returned her greeting and came down the steps toward the car.

"Madre mia, it is *not* a good morning!" the lady in the tonneau said, her smile flashing in contrast to her lugubrious words. "That I should live to see such a day as this! My poor feet! Had not the young Mr. Seymour come in this beautiful car, I must have sat down on the sidewalk to burn like everything else. For not a step more could I have taken. Not one step!"

Beyond the car the studier of tires rose to his feet and smiled at the woman in the back seat—a smile which included Melora and her sister. The young man was the book clerk, Tony Ellis.

"Now, now," he said to the protesting lady, "you know you'd always take one more step as long as it was necessary. This young lady is Miss Melora Cranby, of whom I have told you." He looked at Melora, as if to point up the fact that he had talked about her. "Miss Cranby, my mother, Mrs. Ellis. This second young lady I don't know—" He paused inquiringly.

Cora's dimples were in evidence as she regarded Tony and his mother with interest. Melora introduced her sister, while Quent Seymour unbent from examining a tire to glance at them.

"So you already know Tony? From the bookstore, I suppose. He and I went to school together."

This was an interesting fact, but Melora had other questions to ask. "Quent, what's happening now? The fire isn't up Nob Hill, is it?"

"Things look pretty bad," Quent said, sounding as if he enjoyed the excitement. "I don't see how they'll stop it. All our servants skipped out yesterday. Father sent them off in the carriages in order to get the horses safely away. He just kept the buggy himself. And of course this car."

"Where is your father?" Melora asked.

"Right now he's working on the Mayor's Committee of Fifty. They started out with headquarters in the Hall of Justice on Portsmouth Square, but got burned out last night. They've been moving from one place to another ever since. Father told me to cut some of the best paintings in his collection from their frames and bring them outside the fire lines. So of course I thought of this place." He grinned. "Besides, I was longing to see you, Melora."

Melora threw him a quick look of reproval. This was no time for nonsense and she particularly did not like it with Tony looking on.

"Well, bring them into the house, Quent," she said. "And you, Mrs. Ellis, won't you come in and rest? I think we'll be safe enough here for a while."

Mrs. Ellis accepted with obvious relief, and Tony sprang around the car to open the door and assist his mother to the ground.

"That would be fine," he said gratefully to Melora. "I'm afraid we can't ride any farther with Quent."

"Come on, Cora-Melora," Quent directed, using the old nickname with which he had teased both girls when they were children. "Fall to work here and help get these canvases indoors. Father has threatened to have my head if I don't get this car promptly over to Franklin Hall on Fillmore Street. That's the latest retreat of the Citizens' Committee. All cars are being commandeered for official use."

Quong Sam had informed the rest of the household of Quent's arrival and then returned to be of use himself. Gran and Mrs. Forrest came hurrying out, eager for news. While Tony helped his mother across the sidewalk, Sam and the two girls filled their arms with the art treasures Quent had managed to rescue from the Seymour mansion.

Mrs. Ellis was too heavy for her own small feet and she tottered a little as Gran came down the steps and held out her hand in greeting. Gran remembered Tony from the bookstore and she welcomed his mother like an old friend.

Mrs. Forrest turned at once to Quent. "What is the news, my boy? What's happening to the city now?"

Quent rubbed the back of a hand across his face, leaving a streak of soot in its wake.

"Fire's circling Nob Hill and eating its way up Russian Hill," he said. "We had to go clear around to get through. It's even licking the foot of Telegraph Hill."

"Ah, my family!" Tony's mother cried, and her son consoled her quickly.

"But the dynamiting?" Mrs. Forrest persisted. "Isn't that serving its purpose?"

"Father doesn't think so. He thinks they're just blowing up a lot of places that might be saved. And the fire's skipping right through most of the time. It's even turning back in some places to catch the spots it missed yesterday."

It was Cora who first thought of the practical. "Have you had anything to eat?" she asked, speaking to Quent, but with an eye for Tony.

"Now there's a thoughtful girl!" Quent approved. "Why do I love your sister when she never thinks of such matters? To put it bluntly, I'm starved. And I'm sure Tony and Mrs. Ellis must be too."

Quong Sam heard the words and dumped his armload of paintings unceremoniously upon Melora so that he could find something for the guests to eat.

Gran was talking to Mrs. Ellis. "Of course you're not going on to Golden Gate Park. We have all the room in the world and there's no reason why you and your son shouldn't stay here." She glanced at Quent. "That goes for you and your father too. If you can't get back up Nob Hill tonight, just you come right over here. We'll put you up. After all—" she threw Melora a quick look—"you're practically related to this family."

Melora flushed and became preoccupied with carrying her load into the house. This whole thing had to be stopped, and soon. But she would have to talk to Quent alone first and get his co-operation. Otherwise goodness knew what crazy attitude he might take.

When she came back outside, she sat on the rail of the balcony above the others and watched Sam bring beans and soup to Mrs. Ellis and the two boys.

Mrs. Forrest continued to ply Quent with questions. "I presume the downtown buildings are burned to the ground? The *Mission Bells* offices were in the Call Building. My son edits the magazine, but where he is now, I don't know. Probably in Oakland."

Quent swallowed a mouthful of beans before he replied, "From a distance the Call doesn't look damaged at all. I'm sure it's burned out inside, but it can probably be restored. If San Francisco had built of steel and concrete everywhere, it wouldn't be so bad off now."

"People always said redwood was slow burning," Tony pointed out.

Quent shook his head. "Not under heat like this. Redwood's burning like tinder now."

"What about your father's business, Quent?" Mrs. Forrest went on.

"It's the wrong business to be in," he said lightly. But I expect we'll muddle through. What worries Father most is the loss of all his records. He had to be with the Mayor yesterday, so he sent me downtown to see if I could rescue anything. I couldn't get through the fire lines because his building was already burning.

But I met one of the clerks from the office who had come through on an early ferry."

"Then some of the office force actually reached the building?" Gran asked.

"That's right. They didn't have much time though. This fellow told me they got a big roll-top desk of Father's out of the ground floor office and carted it to a nearby vacant lot where some excavation had been going on. They buried it in a pit and left it there, but it's probably nothing but char. Right now Father's more worried about San Francisco than about business, anyway."

Melora hadn't considered the nature of Uncle Will's business until this moment. To be in insurance at a time like this was certainly not enviable. Everyone would be expecting payment. But Quent in his usual irresponsible way seemed to be taking it pretty lightly.

He bolted the last of his food and stood up. "Thanks for your hospitality," he told Gran. "I'll be getting along now so this car can be put to use. They're still getting the injured out of sections that haven't burned. But we'll probably be back tonight, Father and I, if you'll have us. A good thing Mother and Gwen are in New York. As for me—I wouldn't miss this for anything!"

He waved jauntily, but at the curb he turned back and ran up the steps to where Melora perched on the balcony rail. There was nothing she could do but endure the resounding kiss he planted on her cheek. He was overdoing the performance, but he paid no attention to her annoyance as he ran down the steps and went to crank the car.

When he'd chugged off toward Fillmore Street, Melora became aware of the attention of the others. Tony was watching her curiously. Cora was smiling. Even Gran seemed to be observing her attentively.

"How nice to know that Quent is all right," Cora said.

Melora nodded in agreement. Of course it was nice. Quent was an old friend. But everyone—including Quent—didn't need to make so much of it. Disturbed at what had happened, Melora jumped down from the rail and went inside.

All day the fire raged on. The refugees in the Bonner house roamed restlessly in and out from sidewalk to attic. Only Carlotta Ellis remained rocking in a wicker chair Sam brought out to the porch. She sat there, well wrapped in her own shawls, taking the liveliest interest in the refugee throngs which continued to pour along Washington toward the unburned part of town.

Once Melora sat down on the steps to listen to a conversation Mrs. Ellis was having with an old man who pushed along the street a cart heaped high with his possessions. Both cart and owner smelled strongly of fish and Melora suspected they had had a close association with them in the recent past. The old man spoke Italian volubly and was apparently giving Mama Ellis all the latest news.

When he took up the cart again and pushed it on, Mrs. Ellis explained ruefully to Melora that her brother, Vito Lombardi, who had a fishing boat, and her own Papa, Antonio Lombardi, whose fine restaurant on Telegraph Hill was famous in San Francisco, were not fleeing from the fire at all. They were boasting that they would fight it with casks of wine, if necessary. They would not retreat until the fire touched them with its own flaming fingers. Mama Ellis put her plump hands before her face and shuddered over such foolishness. It was fated, she said, that all the Lombardis should be wiped out in this fire. All except herself and her son. And perhaps her son too would be devoured by the flames. For had he not gone wandering back into the danger zone like a man demented?

Melora assured her that Tony wasn't in the least demented. In fact, she envied him the freedom of a man who could go about at will, without hampering skirts and hampering conventions. He at least might be of some use somewhere, she thought. Even Quent, who so seldom lifted a finger to do anything useful, was working now. While all the women could do was moon about this house and wait for news.

Alec had made a fuss when Gran wouldn't let him go off with Tony to fight the fire, and Mama had come downstairs to object because Gran was apparently taking in refugees right and left. Melora was concerned lest Mrs. Ellis hear the controversy. Fortunately Grandmother was her old, strong self again. Even though her voice sometimes quavered into a high note as she tired, she remained calm.

"I would like to remind you, Addy," she said, "that you were, after all, born in Virginia City, not in San Francisco. And there wasn't the slightest hint of a silver spoon in your mouth. What's more, I am not your only parent. So you needn't go dredging up old plantations and southern blood. It's nice to have them in the background, but when you get down to brass tacks, San Francisco cares only about what a man is as he stands in his boots today. Your father Henry Bonner hadn't a penny to his name when I met him, but he stood very well in his boots as a man. And I was working in a boarding house. If necessary, I can work in one again. This is no time to go swishing around in pearls and superiority, daughter."

Cora ran for Mama's smelling salts, but after that there were no more objections to Mrs. Ellis sitting out there on the balcony chatting with the refugees.

That evening all the men came home. Uncle Will and Quent, with the Oldsmobile still chugging away, despite a breakdown or two and some tire changes.

Cars had their good points, said Uncle Will, springing up the steps as lightly as though he hadn't been working desperately from dawn to dusk. Of course they would never replace the horse, but nothing else could get you around so tirelessly at fifteen or twenty miles an hour. Unfortunately there weren't enough in the city for the great need.

Melora had always been fond of Uncle Will. In fact, one of the things she most regretted about her pretend engagement to his son was the fact that Mr. Seymour had been so genuinely delighted. She had, he'd told her, always been his favorite girl, and nothing could make him happier than to have her become his son's wife.

Uncle Will brought real news of what was going on in the city. He told them what was happening as they all sat around the circular dining table eating an early supper while Quong Sam carried things in from the street kitchen.

Uncle Will said there would soon be relief trains bringing in food enough for everyone. Bread cards were being issued and there'd be no famine. There was water too, though not for bathing. In spite of the fact that San Francisco was cut off from the rest of the country as far as telephone and telegraph went, word of her need had gone out and the Red Cross was already at work.

The Ferry Building had not burned and throngs were still pouring out of the city by that gateway. The Southern Pacific Railroad had been furnishing free meals and free transportation for all those who wanted to leave the disaster area.

Governor Pardee had proclaimed a bank holiday through Saturday, but he'd probably extend it after that to give the banks a chance to get their records in order and prepare to meet the demand for money. For the moment money wasn't much good anyway because there was so little left to buy. The important matters at hand were to halt the fire, minister to the sick and injured and take care of the thousands of refugees. No, he said in answer to a question from Mrs. Forrest, he didn't believe all the wild reports about looting and the shooting of looters. There had been some incidents, of course, but on the whole San Francisco was behaving better than anyone might have expected. There was still no telling, of course, how many were dead in the earthquake and fire, but as far as could be judged the disaster might have been a great deal worse when it came to loss of life.

Tony told dramatically of how he had stood at Geary and Larkin that morning, with the fire burning two blocks away on Leavenworth. There was no doubt at all, he said, that the Cranby house, far over into the fire area, was gone.

After supper Melora stole outside to sit on the back steps alone. She wanted to escape the earthquake and fire talk for a little while. Here on the steps with the dusky garden sloping downhill below her, she could glimpse the bay and see the lights of boats on the water—bright sequins scattered across the dark satin shimmer. To be sure, only a reddish glow marked the sunset. The heavy smoke clouds, reflecting fire, brightened the sky unnaturally. Dynamite shocks still went on, though Uncle Will had said the dynamite gave out from time to time and more had to be brought in.

She knew she had only to turn her head to see the great expanse of flaming sky, with nearby houses on Gough Street standing up in black silhouette. But she did not want to look. She wanted to find a moment of peace where there was something left of the world besides fire and disaster.

She rose and went down into the garden. The color of the grass was no longer visible, but she knew it wore the soft green of April. Across the back of the house a heliotrope vine grew lush and heavy with dark blossoms. And somewhere there was a scent that was not of smoke and cinders, not the hot breath of fire.

She searched it out in a far corner of the garden and knelt on the grass before a flower bed. Roses. Bright red roses, glowing in the dusk, breathing a gentle defiance of the harsh smell on the wind. Heedless of thorns, she bent toward them. She did not hear the footfalls on the grass until they were close and a voice spoke to her in the dim garden.

"I'd forgotten how roses smell," Tony said quietly.

He bent beside her and fragrance was all around them.

"They'll only wither here under the rain of cinders," Tony said. "Shall we cut them and carry them into the house? We need them there."

She shook her head regretfully. "There's no water to spare to keep them alive."

"One rose then. There must be enough for one rose in your room."

He took a metal instrument from his pocket and leaned past her to snip a long-stemmed blossom. "Wire cutters," he said. "I needed them in the streets today. The burned-out part of town is a wilderness of wires to trip you at every hand. Here's your rose."

She took it from him, pleased. She would put the flower beside the statue of Kwan Yin, and her room would be beautiful and fragrant. His gesture touched her and she tried to thank him. But he went on earnestly.

"Is it true then, Melora, that you are engaged to marry Quentin Seymour? That ring on your finger—you always wore gloves when you came into the shop."

She hesitated, seeking the right words. She would tell him the truth. There was no need to fool this young man with her make-believe engagement.

But he seemed to consider her hesitation an answer,

and before she could find words to explain, his tone changed.

"You'll be marrying into an eminent family. The Seymours of Snob Hill. Quent, as always, will have everything handed him on a silver platter, with never an obstacle in his path. My congratulations."

The note of resentment in his voice startled her and her impulse to tell him the truth faded. She knew that many people used that nickname for Nob Hill. But she did not think it applied to the Seymours. Uncle Will was as far from being a snob as anyone could be. He had even insisted on sending his son to a public high school against his mother's wishes. And Quent was an old friend. She did not like to hear Tony dispose of him with such words.

"I'm sorry you feel that way," she said and started toward the house.

He came after her quickly. "If I've offended you, I apologize," he said and opened the door for her with a sweeping gesture.

He behaved, she thought, almost like a character in a play. Perhaps that was what made him a rather exciting person. And since he had apologized she smiled. There was the rose and she couldn't stay indignant with him.

In the dim kitchen Gran was talking to Sam, and Melora held out the rose so she could smell it.

"Tony picked it for me," she said and was uncomfortably aware of the appraising look Gran turned upon him.

Since there could be no lights in the house, everyone went early to bed. Melora, however, felt restless and not at all ready for sleep. As she undressed in the dark she kept thinking about the unexpected contradiction that Tony had so suddenly revealed. Though if it was only jealousy of Quent that had made him speak so—jealousy because of her—she could only feel a little pleased.

She smiled to herself as she put the rose on the shelf beside the statue. Kwan Yin's presence brought again the thought of her father, and she wondered where his ship was now, and if the terrible news about San Francisco had reached him. She wished she might send reassuring thoughts winging in his direction. In a month or so he would be home and with his coming troublesome matters always seemed to clear up.

She turned toward the bed and felt over it in the faintly luminous dark. To her surprise she found her own nightgown laid out upon it and laughed softly. This would be Quong Sam's doing. That bulging carpetbag again! She got into bed thinking guiltily of all the thousands of refugees sleeping in the parks, in the open. Perhaps she shouldn't have undressed tonight. Perhaps there would be a new alarm at any moment and she would have to leap from her bed.

Somewhere at a window a woman was singing sweetly in Italian. Tony's mother perhaps? Mrs. Forrest had said his family was made up of restaurant owners, fishermen, opera singers. Had this plump little woman with the still beautiful face once sung in opera?

The song was like a lullaby. Fear and anxiety stole away and Melora fell deeply asleep.

7

CITY OF ASHES

The fire had crossed Van Ness at more than one point. In the beginning it had burned as far west as their own section, south of Jefferson Square, almost a mile away from the Bonners' house. It had been touch and go with the weary fire fighters holding the blaze close by at Franklin and Clay. Most of the Mission district had gone earlier, and all Market Street, except for the waterfront along the Embarcadero where the fire could be fought by blue jackets manning pumps with water from the bay. It had swept back and forth upon its course and the Nob Hill mansions had gone with the rest. Now on Friday the flames were making a last assault up Russian and Telegraph hills.

A strong stand was being made at Van Ness and the fire was not yet out of control at the points where it had crossed to the west side of the street. The east side had been dynamited practically out of existence.

By late Friday the prospect became constantly more hopeful, and at last came the welcome word from troopers that the fire was checked.

Melora could feel a sort of limpness go through her at the news. There were no great outbursts of joy from the community. Everyone was too worn and weary. Had all this happened in only three days? they asked one another. They seemed to have lived months in these hours.

But now at least apathy fell away and on every hand one heard the words, "What do we do now?" Not in tones of despair, but calmly as people looked about to see what most needed doing. Some four square miles of San Francisco lay in ruin and rubble. Quite an ash pile to clean up, and San Franciscans went to work with a will. What had happened was past—they must now get ready for the future.

Tony made a roundabout trip to Telegraph and Russian hills. His mother's little house on Russian Hill was gone, but the Lombardi Restaurant on Telegraph Hill had been saved and his relatives were living there.

Street kitchens sprang up to enable the populace to eat hot food. No fires were to be built indoors until chimneys had been inspected, and goodness knew when that would be.

On Saturday Quent persuaded Melora's mother that he and Tony should be permitted to escort the two girls on an exploration down Market Street. Only a few fires were smouldering here and there and the ruins were already cooling in that area. There was no danger except from falling walls, and if they stayed in the middle of the street they'd be all right.

"Shouldn't you boys be helping to dig San Francisco out of the rubble?" Gran asked.

"Oh, we'll get to that," Quent said airily. "The mess will be around for a while. But we ought to have a look before we all turn busy beaver."

"If I were young I expect I'd go myself," Gran admitted. "Let them have their exploring, Addy. This is something they'll tell their children about some day."

So Mama gave in. But she put her foot down absolutely about Alec going along. Alec would try to climb about the ruins and she did not mean to let him out of her sight.

Mama was upset today because Gran had accepted some money Mr. Seymour had paid her and agreed to take him and Quent as boarders. Tony and his mother too, and of course Mrs. Forrest, who had still found no way to communicate with her son. In a day or two she would go to Oakland to her friends, but she didn't want to be caught in the crowds that were still jamming the ferries leaving San Francisco.

Hospitality, Gran told Mama, was a fine thing under the proper circumstances. But they all had to be realistic. "Rent" couldn't be steady anyway until the banks opened and they all knew where they stood. Now Addy had to realize that they were in the boarding house business. With one reservation, of course. The tenants might return at any moment—whereupon they might all be out in the cold.

That afternoon the four young people were permitted their walk about the city. Uncle Will was going their way in the car and dropped them off near Market Street. There the two girls had their first real look at the ashes of San Francisco.

What they saw was hard to believe. The City Hall stood a shattered skeleton, with only the top of its dome intact, though strangely enough the figure of Liberty still crowned the pinnacle proudly, with arm and torch lifted high above the wreckage. Quent said the main damage to the building had been from the earthquake, not the fire—a case of shoddy construction which had cheated the people of San Francisco.

Everywhere else stood broken walls, crumbled heaps of brick, tangled wires, lone chimneys. And everywhere the tall, charred spars of telegraph poles standing up like ships' masts in a harbor. At the foot of Market, white and clean and beautiful, stood the Ferry Building. The hands of its clock had stopped at earthquake time, and its flagstaff tilted off at a crazy angle,

but the fire had not reached it and the very sight was a
symbol of hope for the future.

A passageway had already been cleared through the
rubble of Market Street and down its center two
streams moved in opposite directions. One was the line
of cars, wagons and carriages, coming up from the
ferry, bringing supplies, bringing doctors and nurses,
and officials bent on business. The second line, moving endlessly toward the water, was made up for the
most part of refugees, still pouring out of the city,
carrying their thinning loads.

Their own group fitted itself into the refugee line,
walking two abreast. From behind, Cora prodded
Melora.

"I'm glad *we're* not running away!" she cried. "I'm
glad we're staying to see it through!"

"Good for you," Tony approved, but Quent only
smiled and Melora felt an impatience toward him. She
too was glad that Gran was made of pioneer stuff that
didn't run away.

She walked on, ignoring Quent, her eyes upon the
nearby hills. Strange to be able to see them again,
hitherto hidden by buildings, but heart-breaking now
with their crown of ruin. Everywhere glowed the surprise of color. Where Melora had expected to find only
a burned, dead black, bricks glowed pale red, and
lavender and purple.

"How queer," Melora said over her shoulder to Cora
and Tony. "I never thought there'd be color like this."

It was Quent who answered. "The temperatures
were so great that what didn't burn was fused to these
colors."

It was far from quiet here on Market. There was a
ringing of pick and shovel and hammer, the clatter of
rubble being tossed into carts and barrows, voices
shouting. Now and then came the crash of a falling
wall back among the ruins.

They had gone a few blocks down Market when a burly fellow in overalls, loggers' boots and a bowler hat stepped up and collared Quent without ceremony.

"You'll be volunteering, I think, young fellow?" he said, thrusting a shovel into Quent's hands. "Twenty minutes of service is all we ask of every man who passes by. You too, there,"—and he pointed to Tony.

The two boys went to work with a ready will and Melora and her sister found themselves a place where they could sit on a pile of bricks and be out of the moving stream in the middle of the street. The man in the bowler hat went after more "volunteers" and every man put heart and muscle into the effort.

"Of all things, look at that!" Cora cried, and Melora followed the direction of her pointing finger.

Across the street, against the charred front door of a building a man was nailing up a sign crudely lettered. Cora read the words aloud.

> MOVED TO VAN NESS.
> ELEVATOR HERE HAS
> STOPPED RUNNING.

When the sign was secured the fellow turned toward the crowd and saluted with his hammer. There was laughter and a few cheers. Melora saw one man and woman with two small children in tow look at each other and then turn about to walk against the tide of fleeing refugees. Here were two who had changed their minds about flight. There was something hearteningly contagious in the air—a will to survive and build anew.

When the boys had served their stint and the four could go on again, Melora began to look closely at the cross streets for some sign of a landmark. Only the ruin of a business building on Market gave her the answer.

"It's queer not to know where we are because nothing is recognizable and there are no more street signs," she said. "Do you think we could go uphill a little way and see if—if our house—"

"Do you really want to?" Quent asked.

She nodded. "Yes, if the rest of you are willing. This street doesn't look too bad."

Before they left Market Tony called to Melora and Quent who were still ahead. "Wait! Look back up Market!"

Melora saw what he meant. The long diagonal stretched away from them, the ruins of one of the world's great thoroughfares, while above the ashes and destruction rose the green serenity of Twin Peaks. Here and there on distant hills marched a familiar line of eucalyptus trees, and there must be poppies nodding their orange heads in the grass up there. The world still stood, unrocked, unshattered, unscorched.

Now they left Market Street and faced the wilderness of ruins with a lift to their steps. The going was sometimes better, sometimes worse than it looked. Once Melora glanced down at her shoes and long skirts and saw that they were whitened with the powder of lime and brick dust that drifted over everything. Sometimes the girls had to gather up their skirts and climb over piles of debris in the street, sometimes they waited while Tony, his wire cutters out again, helped Quent to clear a path.

Here and there curls of smoke drifted up from some ash heap, and here, with the sounds of Market behind them, the silence was utter and desolate. No human being stirred anywhere. This was truly a dead city. If it had not been for the peculiar jog in the brick steps that had once led up to the Cranby house, they might have had trouble in knowing where it had stood. But a portion of the steps was there—with nothing else beyond but the usual heaps of rubble, the broken sections of wall.

Cora started up the steps with a cry of dismay, but Tony drew her back.

"Don't go up there," he said. "It's better to remember it the way it was."

Tony was right. Always now when Melora tried to remember these steps where she had played as a child, there would be a cavern of rubble beyond them. She would see only sky and the hill, where once the peaked roof had risen above the window of her father's little study. Having looked upon this, she would no longer be able to see Cindy, the rag doll, sitting in the chair beside her bed waiting for her to come home. Now there was no Cindy, no chair, no room, no house.

Only Quent went to the top of the steps and stared down into the ruins. He came down again almost at once, without comment.

"Let's go," he said shortly, and they turned west, picking their way through the cluttered street.

"If it's not too hard to reach," Tony suggested, "I'd like to go past the bookshop—or what's left of it."

The others were willing to try, and the going was not too difficult. They found the bookshop a dark cave between two brick walls. Its front was gone completely and there was nothing overhead. Tony stepped past the heap of masonry that had once been a door and looked inside.

"Wait for me," he said. "I won't be a minute. I just want to see what's left."

They heard him moving about beyond the debris that marked the front of the shop. Once he laughed as bricks tumbled with a clatter all about him. Melora felt her sister's hand tighten on her arm. Then Tony yelled and there was a resounding crash, as if the whole rear of the shop had caved in with a roar of sound. A cloud of dust rose about them, filling the air.

There was no sound from Tony and Quent was already climbing through into the shop, while the girls waited. A moment later the two boys came out together.

Tony's cap was gone and there was brick dust in his hair and a long red scratch down one cheek. He managed to smile as he waved a black lump of something at them.

"Wow!" he said, when he was safely in the middle of the street again. "I didn't expect the whole back wall of the place to fall over like that." He stamped his feet and dusted his clothes. Then he felt gingerly of a lump on the side of his head.

"Mama said we were all to stay where walls couldn't fall on us," Cora said, looking white and a little sick. "You might have been killed!"

Melora said nothing, but her heart was still thumping with the fright he had given them.

Tony shrugged. He was more interested in the blackened object in his hand than in the danger he had barely escaped. As they continued down the street heading toward Van Ness and home, he held it out for them to see.

"Know what this is?"

"I suspect that it used to be a book," Quent said. "Though the deduction is due mainly to the fact that you found it in a bookshop."

"It's still a book," said Tony triumphantly. He fluttered the pages under Melora's nose. "Books aren't the easiest thing in the world to burn. The covers are gone and the outer pages, but look—you can read the rest. Melora—do you know what book it is?"

The edge of the page was brown and crumbling, but print stood out black against white and she needed to read only a few lines:

In I got bodily into the apple barrel, and found there was scarce an apple left; but, sitting down there in the dark, . . . I had either fallen asleep, or was on the point of doing so, when a heavy man sat down with rather a clash close by. . . . I was just about to jump up when the man began to speak. It was Silver's voice, and, before I had heard a dozen words, . . . I understood that the lives of all the honest men aboard depended upon me alone.

Cora started to speak, but Melora was first.

"Of course I know," she said. "It's *Treasure Island*."

Even Quent, who was no steady reader, glanced at the scorched page and nodded. "Best adventure story I ever read!"

Tony forgot the other two to walk beside Melora. "I couldn't help thinking about Stevenson the other night when I stood on Russian Hill and watched the downtown buildings burning all around Portsmouth Square."

She knew what he meant. Once Robert Louis Stevenson had lived for a time in San Francisco—in fact, his widow still lived on Russian Hill. In bygone days Stevenson had haunted Portsmouth Square, sitting for long hours in the sun while he talked to seamen, getting a taste for the South Seas, and a curiosity that would eventually send him sailing to those far islands. After his death a monument had been erected in that very square, topped by a golden galleon, its sails billowing full with wind as it sailed upon lapping waves.

"The *Hispaniola*," Melora said. "My father used to take me down there sometimes when I was a little girl —when Cora was still too young to come along. My father's a sailor, you know, and like Stevenson he loved stories of the sea. I used to play around the

Stevenson monument, while Papa talked to whoever came along. Tony, do you suppose it's gone— that little galleon? I hate to think of that."

Quent heard her words. "There can't be anything but ruin left of Portsmouth Square. The fire ringed it in completely."

"No fire could hurt that galleon," Tony said confidently.

"Why not?" Quent asked. "You mean it's stuff that wouldn't burn?"

Tony laughed and shook his head. "I'm sure the ship wasn't there to burn. Don't you know the legend? They say at times when the night is clear and San Francisco sleeps, the *Hispaniola* soars away with its sails filled and all the seaways for its home. So why wouldn't it escape when the fire came too close and return when it was safe again?"

"I'd like to think that," Melora said quietly.

Tony handed Melora the book with a quick gesture. "It's for you. A souvenir of the fire."

She took the blackened volume in her hands gravely. "Thank you very much. I'll treasure this."

Quent quickened his pace as if he'd grown suddenly impatient, and Cora murmured that she was tired.

They were all weary enough of such difficult walking by the time they reached Van Ness, and without ceremony Cora dropped down on a stretch of unbroken curb, sighing. Melora followed her example, and Quent found a place beside them. Only Tony stood up, looking along the street.

Van Ness, marking the western boundary of the fire line, was alive with activity. On most of its western edge the mansions still stood proudly. Along the east spread wreckage left by fire and dynamite, but men were clearing rubble away and here and there along the sidewalk shacks were springing up. These were not refugee camps, but individual business enterprises.

Beside one of them a young bootblack was working hard and gentlemen in oddly assorted attire were having their boots freed of dust. A mailman plodded along the west side of the street, distributing letters. Quent said he'd heard that the post office had been saved and desultory mail service had been resumed. Any sort of mail was being accepted, stamps or no.

Quent grimaced. "Sooner or later I suppose we'll have to get to work ourselves, Tony."

Tony was interested in the business activity of the street and a thoughtful look had come into his eyes.

"I'd like to try something more imaginative than a pick and shovel," he said. "This gives me an idea. Now if I can just locate Mr. Gower—"

But he would not tell them the details of his sudden notion, though Cora teased him, and since the afternoon was growing late, they went on toward home.

8

"HOW DO YOU KNOW?"

They reached home to find Quong Sam cooking supper on the laundry stove in the street. He had gained the help of neighbors to bring the stove out and had built a protecting lean-to around it of salvaged boards and corrugated iron. Sam, clearly, was in his element. He liked nothing better than to boss the family. These days no one suggested menus to him. Sam did as he pleased and so far he had managed to feed them. At the moment a huge wash boiler sat atop the laundry stove, steaming with a savory stew.

Cora sniffed hungrily. Nothing ever impaired her appetite. "What is it, Sam? And when do we eat?"

"Palace special," said Sam, stirring the mixture with a big wooden spoon. "Pletty soon eat."

Alec, who hovered nearby, with Smokey at his heels, explained. "He put everything in it. Lima beans and canned soup and corn and spaghetti. And that funny fish stuff of yours too, Melora."

"Oh, no!" Melora wailed. "Not my caviar!"

"You no likee, you no eatee," said Sam severely and no one offered further criticism.

They'd have been willing to sit on the curb or the steps with their assorted bowls of the "Palace" mixture. But Quong Sam was one who believed in doing

things in proper fashion. When he was ready he
shooed them inside to sit about the round table in the
dining room. It was a dark room and it would have
been nice to have a fire on the hearth, since the house
was chilly and draughty from broken windows. But of
course that wasn't allowed.

At least Sam's hot "caviar stew," as Melora named
it, brought grateful warmth and nourishment. There
was even bread again, as Mrs. Forrest and Mama,
whose cough was better, had gone to stand in a bread
line and had brought home two loaves.

What a tableful they were, Melora thought, looking
about as the others chattered and exchanged experiences of the day. Those she knew best seemed most
like strangers. If anyone had told her when she left
Chicago—how long ago that seemed!—that she'd
shortly be eating such a meal and listening to her
mother talk about standing in a bread line, she'd have
found the suggestion too fantastic for belief.

Mrs. Ellis seemed so plainly foreign, yet she was
fitting herself comfortably into their midst. And just
across the table, with Cora hanging on his every word,
was Tony.

Quent, placed at Melora's side by Sam, wasn't saying much, just eating heartily. But she knew him well
enough so that she could sense his amusement over
Cora's remarks on the subject of "beautiful"
ruins. And she did not miss the sardonic look he gave
her sister when she fluttered long lashes at Tony.

Apparently Tony's interest worried Mama, for she
drew Melora aside right after supper. In the tower section adjoining the parlor and overlooking the bay, was
a "cozy corner" which had been lavishly furnished by
the Hoopers in the recently popular Moorish manner.

Mama sank onto the soft pillows on the window seat
and drew Melora down beside her. "Everything has
been so confused since you got back, dear. There's

been no time for a visit. Later I must hear all about Chicago and how the wedding went. And we must discuss the future too—your marriage to Quent. When I think of all that lovely material I'd bought for your new clothes going up in flames—!"

Melora started to speak, but her mother went on.

"Right now I want to talk about your sister. I'd never have dreamed that your grandmother would simply open the house to strangers without even consulting me. And now this—this unusual young man is making eyes at Cora. You can see the child is impressed. He's the type to flirt with every pretty girl who comes along, but she's too young to understand that. No one that much older has ever treated her like this before, so of course it's going right to her head."

"I think you're worrying about nothing, Mama," Melora said a little stiffly. "Cora can be a bit of a flirt too. You know how Gran says she's a throwback to the old-fashioned southern belle. Besides, as you say, she's much too young for Tony."

"She won't believe that herself," Mrs. Cranby said. "I just don't like this—this leveling of classes. It can bring nothing but trouble and unhappiness."

Melora played with a fuzzy ball on the dark red drapery fringe. "Tony is really very nice when you get to know him."

Mama shook her head in distaste. "I have no desire to know him. Why, his mother was on the stage. She was an opera singer—Lotta Lombardi. She told me so herself. What surprises me, Melora, is that you should be in league against me like this."

Melora gave the fringe a quick flick. "No one's against you, Mama. In a few days Tony and his mother will probably move away, so you're worrying unnecessarily."

"With your grandmother's plans, I don't know. Anyway, dear, do try to keep an eye on your sister. If you see her alone with that young man, go and join them."

Her mother reached out to pat her arm in a soothing gesture.

"The one bright spot in all this, as far as I am concerned, is that you and Quent have settled things between you. Even when I was sure the house was coming down around my ears, I thought thankfully of that. I knew you'd be taken care of no matter what happened. You've made a wise choice, my dear."

Melora squirmed and longed to blurt out the truth.

"Have you ever thought," she asked limply, "that Quent is rather lazy, that he lacks ambition and that he always clowns instead of taking things seriously?"

There was shock in her mother's eyes. "Melora! What a dreadful way to speak of one you love. Never in all my life would I have spoken so of your father."

Her indignation was so great, her lack of understanding so complete, that Melora smiled helplessly.

"I'll try to keep an eye on Cora, but I still don't think you need to worry," she assured her mother as she rose from the cushioned seat.

Too disturbed to stay with her mother longer, Melora went out the front door. Gran was seated in a chair beside Mrs. Ellis. These two who were so different could chat with each other in absorbed interest. Gran certainly had no such notions as Mama did about "classes."

When her grandmother saw Melora she excused herself to Tony's mother and left her chair.

"Come for a walk with me, Granddaughter. I've not been away from the house all day."

"You're doing too much," Melora said. "You'll wear out your strength."

Her grandmother smiled. "Maybe I'm tired, but I haven't felt so much alive in years."

Melora expected her to turn toward the park,

perhaps climb to a high place where she could view the ruined part of the city. But Gran walked resolutely west toward the section the fire had not reached. By late afternoon fog had rolled in from the bay and now hung low overhead, touching the hilltops, but not yet engulfing the streets. Fog horns coughed hoarsely out on the water and the clean touch of dampness on the wind was refreshing.

As they walked along past street kitchens, greeting strangers with the easy friendliness disaster had bred, Melora began to speak of what she had seen that day.

"It's only a ghost city now, Gran. There's nothing left but a shell. Our house is just steps and emptiness. When I remember—"

"Don't look back except to remember the good things," Gran said. "Let's have no truck with unhappy ghosts."

"Mama is trying to make *now* be exactly like the past," Melora pointed out. "And I don't think you can do that either."

"Of course you can't. But a lot of people aren't going to accept the change all this will bring. At least not right away. Melora, this will be harder for your mother than for the rest of us. She hasn't our advantage."

"What do you mean—advantage?"

"Why," said Gran, "having hard things happen to us young. Plenty happened to me and my family when the Yankees burned down our home. And when my first husband was killed in battle."

Melora covered her grandmother's hand where it lay upon her arm. Mostly she forgot about that very young husband whom Gran had been married to less than a year. When a husband was mentioned, it was always the children's grandfather, Henry Bonner, and Melora knew how much Gran had loved him. Now, for the first time, she had a glimpse of an old pain, and of a growing, a maturing that must have resulted from it.

They paused at a side street looking out toward the bay where fog already hid the opposite shore. When Gran spoke again it was in the same calm voice.

"Like me, you've lost everything while you are still young. Though not as much as I lost. Because you are young you are resilient. And because of what has happened you will be stronger all your life when you have to face trouble. Your mother thought leaving the Bonner place was hard, but she doesn't know what real hardship is. So all this is going to be harder for her than for the rest of us. We'll have to give her time. She needs your father just now."

Melora nodded silently. They all needed him.

It was growing chilly and Melora shivered, but Gran stood where she was, looking off toward the water. For one so small and slight, there was weight to her when she chose to stand her ground.

"What about this marriage to Quent?" Gran asked abruptly.

"What do you mean?" Melora was startled by the sudden question.

"Sometimes," Gran said, "I wonder if you're really serious about Quent."

Always Gran saw through make-believe, Melora thought. Others might be fooled, but never Gran.

"What if I'm not serious?" Melora asked.

Gran's gaze seemed to look past any guard her granddaughter might have worn. "Your mother is exceedingly pleased about it. You know that, I think?"

"Of course she's pleased! She thinks it will be fine for me to live in a mansion on Nob Hill where I'll be waited on by butlers and have fifty ball gowns."

"Might have been at that," said Gran. "But she's maybe overlooking one little fact. The old Nob Hill is gone. And so in all probability is the Seymour fortune. Have you considered Will Seymour's business?"

"Insurance, you mean?" Melora recalled Quent's comments earlier.

"Exactly. I'll be surprised if this doesn't wipe out every penny Will has, or that Quent will inherit."

"But Uncle Will doesn't seem worried. He's been working on the Mayor's Committee as if he hadn't anything else to do."

"Naturally," said Gran. "We all do what's necessary first. So must you, Melora."

"I don't understand—" Melora began.

"If you weren't sure about Quent, you shouldn't have tampered with so serious a matter. It's unlike you. But since you have this is no time to upset your mother and throw Quent over when the Seymours are suffering such a loss. I hope you will think about that. Well, let's be getting home before Sam locks us out for the night."

She turned to start back and Melora fell into step beside her.

"But Gran—" she protested, and then broke off because there seemed to be nothing she could say. Her grandmother's words had opened up a dismaying possibility she had not glimpsed until this moment. It had never occurred to her that anyone would think the engagement was being broken because the Seymour fortune might be gone. Even Mama, who so wanted luxury for her daughter, would expect her to stand on certain principles.

Her grandmother spoke more gently. "Youth is a time for doing foolish things. We all have our turn at it. But just you hang onto Quent, even if he hasn't a fortune behind him. I think he'll do all right one of these days when he grows up."

"Gran, it isn't that!" Melora wailed, feeling a frantic need to escape from what seemed to be a closing trap. "The whole thing was a joke. Quent planned it him-

self. To get everyone to stop match-making. He's always full of pranks. He'll never grow up. Not that it
isn't my fault too."

She was aware of the long look her grandmother
gave her, but now they were nearly home.

They found Quong Sam padding about in his
slippers, locking things up for the night. The earthquake rule was still to bed at sundown, up with the
daylight. He grumbled under his breath as they came
in and they tiptoed up the stairs together, subdued by
the silence of the house.

"He looks ready to scold," Gran whispered. "We'd
better be good and go right to bed."

Melora kissed her grandmother's cheek and went to
her own floor. It was pitch dark and she had to feel
her way along the paneled wall of the upper balcony.
To her surprise, she found her door open. As she
stepped in a voice spoke to her from the window seat.
She saw the outline of her sister's head against the dim
light.

"I've been waiting for you," Cora whispered.
"Please—could we talk a little?"

"Of course," Melora said. There was something rapt
and dreamy about Cora's tone that warned her. She sat
on the window seat, waiting.

"When you're terribly happy you can endure almost
anything, can't you, Mellie?" Cora began.

Mellie. The old name out of their childhood, when
"Melora" had been too hard for a baby sister to say.

"What do you mean?" Melora asked.

"Well, like you and Quent, for instance. I mean
since everything's decided and you've got each other
and you're sure—the city can come down in ruins and
you can lose everything, yet still it doesn't matter.
You're happy. You've still got the important thing."

"I don't know that it's quite like that," Melora said.

Cora went on. "Mellie, what do you think of Tony Ellis?"

So Mama had been right. It would be necessary to move carefully now, say the right thing.

"He seems nice enough." Melora tried to speak casually. "But don't forget that there's always an appeal about someone who is different from the people we're accustomed to. They're sure to seem—well, more exciting." That was true. She had recognized it herself.

"He is different and exciting, isn't he? Not like any boy I've ever known. He does such surprising things. Little thoughtful things that make you feel you're— sort of special."

Melora sat very still. She knew her cheeks were warm and was glad Cora could not see them in the dark.

"Oh, boys usually like me and I've had crushes before," Cora went on in a rush. "But this is different. Mellie, how does it feel to be truly in love? How do you *know?*"

Melora choked back the sharp "How should I know?" that rose to her lips. "I don't think that's anything you can put into words," she faltered.

"But you and Quent . . . I mean you knew him all those years. You played together as children and fought like anything. So what made you change? How did you feel inside that made you know you'd begun to love him?"

"I don't know that I do know. I don't know how anybody can ever be sure."

She heard Cora's gasp of dismay. "Oh, no, Melora! I don't believe that. You loved him enough to tell him you'd marry him. And you couldn't have changed your mind since then. That's not like you. Why, Mama would—"

Melora cut in. "Don't you say a word to Mama. This is something for Quent and me to settle first. I'm just saying this to let you know that—that feelings aren't always to be trusted. Anyone can get giddy at times and fall in love with love. For goodness' sakes, Cora, don't go fancying yourself in love with Tony Ellis. You don't know him at all. He's too old for you."

"He's not as much older as Papa is older than Mama. But don't get so excited about it. I thought I could talk to you, but I see it was a mistake. You sound just like Mama. And I can guess how she'd feel about this. Don't *you* go running to her either!"

Melora could sense the pride and hurt that choked her sister's voice as Cora started for the door.

"I'm sorry," she said. "I'm not so unfeeling as you think, I just don't want to see you get hurt. I don't believe Tony Ellis means anything by his little gallantries. He just wants us to like him. We mustn't let it go to our heads."

"We?" said Cora, pausing with her hand on the doorknob.

"He's been nice to me too. But run along to bed now. You'll see things more clearly in the morning."

Cora said good night somewhat distantly and went down the hall to her own room.

Preparing for bed, Melora hoped that she too would see matters more clearly in the morning. One thing she had to figure out was how to face this suspicion that if she and Quent put a stop to their joke at this time, everyone would think she was throwing him over because of the lost Seymour fortune. There must be some way around that.

9

"LET'S GET GOING!"

Melora lay on the hard mattress of the strange bed and listened to the night's silence, unable to fall asleep. There were no longer the noises of a city on fire. She could close her eyes. The danger was over.

She wished her father were home. There'd always been a warm, understanding friendship between them. He never hurried to condemn, but always listened sympathetically and tried to weigh all the aspects so she could see more clearly and decide for herself. Everyone else would tell her what to do. Papa would help her to find her own way.

Earlier that day, searching out books to carry to her room, she had picked up a tablet of paper and a pencil as well. She missed her diary, left in her suitcase in Oakland, and had thought of writing some of her experiences to her father. Now there was time for that.

A candle stood in a china holder on the table. Surely it would be all right to light one little candle, now that the fire danger was over.

She slipped out of bed, shivering at the sudden chill, and reached absently for her wrapper. Then she remembered and put on her coat. There were matches beside the candle and she lit it, feeling as though the

94

scratch of stick on emery was loud enough to rouse everyone in the house.

The pointed yellow plume flickered and then burned high and straight. In the dim light she could see Kwan Yin smiling at her benevolently, and the red rose in the vase wilting for lack of water.

Melora seated herself at the table. The charred volume of *Treasure Island* lay beside the writing tablet and she picked it up idly, leafed through it. Always this book would remind her of Tony—even after he was completely gone from her life.

She reached for the pencil and began to write to her father. Not about Quent, or about Cora or Tony. Such things could only be put into spoken words. But there was release in writing about what had happened in these last few days. About the fears and discomforts, of course. The fear she had felt for the family until she was reunited with them. The way at first everyone froze at an earth tremor they'd have laughed off before. And the longing for water—gallons and gallons of fresh clean water. Somehow being hopelessly dirty was one of the most distressing feelings of all.

But she did not intend this to be a letter of complaint, so she wrote of hopeful things too. She told him about the walk through the ruined streets of San Francisco, and of the feelings she had that the city would build again and that its people were strong and courageous. Perhaps this meant a new life for San Francisco's citizens, as well as for the city. Already there were changes. . . .

Only then did she begin to write about Tony Ellis and his mother, who were now staying under this very roof. She had finished no more than a paragraph, however, when a tap at the door startled her.

"Who is it?" she called softly.

The door opened a crack and Quong Sam's round face appeared in the opening.

"Whassa matta you burn candle?" he demanded. "You wantchee p'lice come this house, lock evelybody up?"

"Oh, Sam, don't you suppose they've relaxed the regulations a little by now? I'm only writing a letter to Papa."

"No writee letta now. You no go bed, Missy M'lory, I go tellum you gran'ma."

Melora knew that there was never any winning an argument with Quong Sam. If it was something he felt strongly about, you might as well give up because he never would.

But on this matter of the candle he was undoubtedly right.

"I'll blow it out," she promised, but before she could puff up her lips and bend toward the flame, Sam pattered swiftly into the room, his hands behind his back.

"Bling plesent," he said and dropped something on the bed. Then off he went to the door and closed it softly behind him.

In the flickering candlelight she recognized the object on the bed. Of all things, it was Cindy, the well-worn rag doll of her childhood. Gran had made Cindy for her long ago. Sam must have seen her there in Melora's room, and picked her up.

Melora blew out the candle and got back into bed. This time Cindy's lumpy, stuffed hand was between her fingers, the doll beside her. And somehow her presence was comforting.

During the next few days the tempo of life quickened as San Francisco dug into its ashes and began the work of recovery. An overhead trolley was being installed on Market Street, cable cars had appeared out on Fillmore, and everywhere business men counted their losses, shrugged them aside and considered how to build anew. There would be the insurance money, they told one another. Everything would be all right.

There had been good news for Mrs. Forrest. All the newspapers were running personal columns to enable friends and relatives to recover touch with one another. "Your husband is camping on southeast corner of post-office grounds," one item read. Another: "You will find May Peck at Camp Forrest at Fell and Laguna Streets." Among the listings was one inquiring for Nell Forrest, letting her know that her son was safely with friends in Oakland. "Join me," the message pleaded.

So Mrs. Forrest had dusted her clothes as well as she could and accepted Mr. Seymour's offer of a lift to the ferry in the Oldsmobile. She promised Mama before leaving that the first thing she would do was send a cable to Captain Cranby to let him know his family was safe.

There was still no running water, no electricity, no gas, no fires to be built in chimneys, but the relief trains were hurrying to the aid of the city now, bringing supplies and money from all across the country. President Theodore Roosevelt had seen to it that the large donation raised went into the hands of the city's trusted ex-mayor, Mr. James D. Phelan. There was food for everyone and the Relief Committee was organized to dole it out. Clothes for the refugees were coming in too and there were various relief stations set up in Golden Gate Park, as well as all across the city. It was startling to see Nob Hill ladies with pearls about their necks and diamonds on their fingers dressed in dowdy refugee clothes as they stood in bread lines. Gentlemen were getting into overalls, red flannel shirts and loggers' boots. There was work to be done in San Francisco and no one was loafing on the job. Tony and Quent helped with the others.

On Sunday more people attended church services than ever before. In contrast to last Sunday,

which had been Easter, "church" was where you
found it. Services were held in all the parks, on the
steps of ruined churches, on street corners.

On Wednesday, one week after the fire, Tony Ellis
asked the girls to come and visit him at his "business
establishment" on Van Ness. Mama had given up ob-
jecting to unconventional behavior for the moment and
in the afternoon the two girls set out for Van Ness.
Alec was permitted to come too, though with the
warning that they weren't to let him out of sight. So,
too, was Smokey, whose leg had healed. Alec was joy-
ful over the good news that the school term had been
declared ended and that everyone would be promoted
automatically to the next grade. He was eager to make
side forays and had to be restrained from climbing over
every pile of bricks, or through any webbing of wire
that drew him from the main road.

Since the night when Cora had waited in her room,
Melora had been conscious of a faint restraint between
herself and her sister. Cora evidently regretted giving
her confidence so trustingly, and Melora was torn between the troubled sense that she had failed her sister,
and another feeling that she did not want to look at
too closely. A feeling which was tied up with her own
interest in Tony Ellis.

Today Van Ness was a startling sight. The buckled
pavement still bore witness to the earthquake's wrench-
ing. Nevertheless, the thoroughfare bustled with carts,
carriages, wagons and cars, while pedestrians thronged
the sidewalks. The very air resounded with pounding
and hammering and the squeaking of saws.

Melora paused before a new business establishment
made of one green window shutter and several bill-
boards with the gaudy pictures turned out. A smiling
young woman was selling sacks of candy to passers-
by and behind her hung a sign:

The cow is in the hammock,
The cat is in the lake,
The baby's in the garbage can,
What difference does it make?
There is no water, and still less soap,
We have no city, but lots of hope.

"Nothing left but candied violets," the girl told
Melora cheerfully. "Like some? The price is high,
but they taste real good."

Melora studied the remaining change in her purse
and cautiously bought a small quantity that would give
them all a taste. Caviar and candied violets and a city
in ruins! But there was no need for anything to make
sense. There was an exciting activity in the air that was
contagious. Without stopping to draw a deep breath
or count her losses, San Francisco was already reaching for the stars.

They all took bits of the violet-colored flowerets and
Melora enjoyed the hard, sugary texture and the odd
taste that was like the scent of violets.

"Look," Cora said, nudging Melora's arm. "There's
Mr. Gower across the street. Let's go over and see if
he knows what Tony is up to."

They waited for a cartload of rubble to go past and
then hurried after Mr. Gower, Alec and Smokey
trotting at their heels. He tugged spasmodically at his
gray mustache and peered through gold-rimmed spec-
tacles at the front of a house on the west side of the
street.

When Melora spoke he turned and reached for a hat
that wasn't there. The futile gesture seemed to return
him to the present and he smiled apologetically.

"Good morning," he said. "No—it's afternoon, isn't
it? I find it difficult to keep track of the days just now,
let alone the hours. I trust all your family are safe,
Miss Melora?"

"We're fine," Melora told him. "Did you know that Tony Ellis and his mother are staying with us at the Bonner house for the time being?"

Mr. Gower drew a scrap of paper from an inner pocket and showed it to her. Apparently Tony had left a notice at the remains of the old store, giving both his present address and an announcement of where he was "doing business."

"Do you know what this is all about?" Mr. Gower asked. "What possible business can the boy be engaged in?"

Melora shook her head, but Cora smiled knowingly. "He hinted to me, Mr. Gower. But I'm not supposed to tell. He said we'd have to come see for ourselves."

So Tony had made a point of confiding in Cora, Melora thought, faintly piqued. She offered Mr. Gower a candied violet which he accepted gravely, and they all walked on together. They discovered Tony even before they reached him, two blocks down Van Ness. He stood on a wooden packing case, head and shoulders above the crowd, and he was behaving in a way that Melora was sure would have shocked her mother. Plainly Tony Ellis was hawking some sort of wares and he was doing it with great zest and an engaging charm.

"That one!" said Mr. Gower, quickening his steps. "What will he be up to next? I've told his mother a thousand times that he'll never make a bookman. What he wants to do, of course, is go on the stage, but his mother is terribly against that. She feels that because Tony will inherit her share in the business, he ought to work in it. But he does some very strange things. As his father did before him, I must admit."

They could see as they drew near that an amused group had gathered about Tony's packing case to listen and watch. Melora gasped in recognition as he held up a blackened object. Goodness! He had dug more half-burned books from the shop and was actually selling them!

"Step up, step up, ladies and gentlemen!" his voice beguiled them. "If you're weary of theater parties and rich dinners, why not stay home tonight and read a good book?"

Laughter. Tony bowed and went on.

"Of course you can't be sure of the beginning of the story, which may well be missing, and you can't be sure how it ends. But don't judge a book by its cover. What am I bid, ladies and gentlemen, for this handsome, this truly unique copy of *The Virginian?* Even if you can't read, or have no time, due to present social engagements, you can take home a fine souvenir of the great San Francisco fire."

A silver coin flew through the air and chimed among others in a battered tin pan at Tony's feet and the "book" changed hands. Before he could reach toward the pile beside him for another, Mr. Gower squirmed his way through the crowd with the girls behind him. His indignation was so great that he could hardly speak for sputtering.

"You—you're not s-selling this—this junk? Get down at once, sir! You are disgracing the name of Gower & Ellis. What is the meaning of this?"

He gestured and Melora saw that Tony had placed a conspicuous and neatly lettered sheet of cardboard against his packing case. She had to choke back a laugh as she read it.

TEMPORARY SITE
OF GOWER & ELLIS,
Famed Booksellers of San Francisco

Not at all disconcerted, Tony glanced briefly at his father's partner and then past him to the girls. He gave them all a merry salute, but he did not obey the order to descend from his stand. An open car had just drawn up in the street opposite and some ladies with motoring veils tied over huge hats stood up to see what was going on.

"What have we here?" Tony cried dramatically, and the crowd turned to look. "Rubberneckers, I do believe. These clean, well dressed ladies and gentlemen are not refugees, I think, but have come to witness our misery. Naturally they will be happy to pay well for such magnificent souvenirs as I have here." He stooped to gather up a half dozen volumes.

The gentleman who was driving the car reached hastily to release the brake, but Tony stopped him.

"Wait, sir! This is for the Earthquake Fund, you know."

The good-natured crowd took up the cry and the car was quickly surrounded. "Give to the Earthquake Fund!" several voices shouted and the men in the car hastily brought out bills in exchange for half-burned books and the car went on.

Even then Tony did not get down from his packing case to talk to Mr. Gower. "It's for a good cause, sir," he said by way of explanation. "The Fund needs every penny it can raise, and I thought this a good way to dispose of what is otherwise pure waste. But I need some help at this job. Would you young ladies like to step up and assist me?"

Melora shrank from the thought of getting up there in front of the crowd. But Cora presented herself at the foot of Tony's perch.

"I'll help if you can get me up there!" she cried.

Tony leaped down from the case and offered his clasped hands as a step for Cora's small shoe, boosting her onto the box. Then he sprang up beside her and cried, "Let's get going, San Francisco!"

The presence of a pretty girl handing out books and taking the money increased the fun and coins began to chink into the pan at a great rate. Even though such behavior was not for her, Melora rather envied the easy manner so natural to Cora and to Tony too.

Mr. Gower coughed disapprovingly. "This matter seems to be out of my hands. If you'll excuse me, Miss Melora, I'll continue my search. I understand a number of businesses are already renting space in these houses along Van Ness. I might as well consider the possibility. When the banks open again and when the insurance companies pay up . . ." He did not finish, but made again the gesture of reaching to tip a non-existent hat and went back across the street.

Melora watched the two on the packing case. There was certainly something of the actor about Tony as he stood high above the crowd, commanding attention. Cora had only to be herself, gay and a little saucy, and the crowd loved her. A red hair ribbon (from the depths of Sam's bottomless carpetbag) now stood out stiffly at the back of her neck, holding the long hair that cascaded down her back. Her sister's eyes did not meet Melora's, but Tony made no attempt to avoid her gaze.

In fact, as she stood there watching, elbowed by the crowd, she had the feeling that Tony was performing mainly for her. Now and then his dark, laughing glance swept her face and she knew that he was as completely aware of her as she was of him. Even some of his jokes seemed to be made for her benefit. There was a reference to a rose blooming in the fire, and another to Stevenson. It was exhilarating to be played to in this fashion, but also faintly disturbing.

After a few moments she turned away and slipped through to the outer rim of the crowd. She was thinking of Tony altogether too much these days. She didn't want to find herself behaving as Cora did. He was such a quicksilver person. Just when she thought she knew him, he changed before her eyes.

What she needed, she told herself firmly, was something to occupy her time. Something that would be of use to San Francisco.

"Let's get going, San Francisco!" Tony had said, and quite plainly that was already the watchword on all sides. There was an enormous amount of work to be done, yet here she was still a mere sight-seer. She couldn't pick up a shovel and help to dig out the ruins, but there ought to be something—

"Miss." A man touched her elbow and she turned. "Is that your little brother over there? That wall don't look so steady to me."

She had forgotten Alec was there. She did not wait for the man to finish, but flew toward the wreckage of a dynamited house where Alec was balanced precariously atop a crumbling wall. Smokey yapped excitedly at its foot.

"Come down from that wall!" she cried to Alec, her heart in her mouth.

He turned his freckled face in her direction, looking a mischievous as Cora. "Aw, Sis, I'm all right! Everything's just as solid up here as—as—" A brick slipped from beneath his foot and he had to wave his arms wildly to keep his balance. But he lost neither his grin nor his confidence.

Melora stepped into the rubble beneath the leaning wall. Alec must be made to come down, if she had to go after him herself.

But rescue came from an unexpected quarter. Tony jumped down from the packing case and ran toward them. He caught Melora unceremoniously by the arm and pulled her away from the wall, shouting to Alec.

"Jump out toward the grass! That whole wall's going to topple over in about two minutes. Jump away from it, boy!"

Tony wasn't fooling and Alec, first calling to

Smokey to get away, jumped onto the scorched remains of a lawn on the far side. He stumbled and fell, then got up and ran toward the street. A moment later the tottering mass of bricks gave way and the whole thing crashed inward, raising a great cloud of brick and lime dust.

Melora felt her knees go limp and she began to tremble. Tony looked at her in concern.

"Are you all right?"

She braced herself. "It was my fault. I forgot to watch him. If anything had happened—"

"Don't think about that," Tony said. "Suppose I take the money over to the Fund place—then I'll see you all home."

She tried to tell him it wasn't necessary, but he hurried off to get the money.

Cora had watched the whole swift incident from the packing case and now she joined her sister and brother.

"Oh, Alec, why don't you be careful?" she wailed.

Alec looked sheepish and pulled at Smokey's ear.

When Tony rejoined them and they started for home, Cora almost skipped as she walked. She was still excited and gay and it seemed as though she were almost driven by a need to attract Tony's attention. But Tony walked at Melora's side and only now and then did he turn a glance her sister's way.

10

OUT OF A TRUNK

At the Bonner place there was fresh activity around the laundry stove kitchen on the curb. Quong Sam had given way to Mrs. Ellis and was being indoctrinated into the mysteries of cooking Italian spaghetti. When Carlotta Ellis saw the young people coming down the sidewalk she waved a long-handled spoon at them. Papa Lombardi, who was Tony's grandfather, and Uncle Vito Lombardi, had come down earlier from the restaurant on Telegraph Hill, and brought with them all the makings for spaghetti. She put the spoon down to show them a length of crusty Italian bread. It was slightly stale, she said—but no matter. The young had good teeth.

"Too bad you missed them," she told Tony. "Uncle Vito has not been out to fish since the fire, but he goes tomorrow. And then perhaps we will have fish too."

"That's wonderful," Melora said warmly and glanced at Tony. He looked neither pleased nor interested, but ignored the bubbling pan of spaghetti sauce and turned to a car which stood at the curb beyond the kitchen.

"Whose car is that?" he asked.

Sam answered him. "Blingee tlunk. Him inside alleady."

"A trunk?" said Cora blankly.

"It must be my trunk from Oakland!" Melora cried and ran up the steps and into the house.

Sure enough, her trunk and suitcase were standing in the dim hall at the foot of the stairs. So Mrs. Forrest had apparently been able to recover them. Mama was in the parlor talking to Mrs. Forrest, and she sighed as the girls appeared.

"I never know what they're doing any more. This whole experience has been so disrupting to any sort of routine."

"Disrupting is a good word for it," Mrs. Forrest said dryly. "Good afternoon, girls. I thought you'd like to have your things as soon as possible, Melora. My son Howard brought them over today in his car. He's in the drawing room now, talking to Mr. Seymour and your grandmother. About some business venture, I'm sure."

Melora had met Mrs. Forrest's son only a few times and remembered him with respect. As editor of one of California's more important magazines, he knew all sorts of famous and successful people, and was quite well-known himself.

"Hurry and open your trunk, Melora," her sister pleaded. "Maybe there'll be something in it I can wear. Goodness knows I need a change."

"Perhaps you can help your grandmother out too," Mrs. Cranby said. "Unfortunately, I'm not as thin as the rest of you. I don't know what I'm going to do for clothes."

"Our friends in Oakland sent something over for you," Mrs. Forrest assured her. "Perhaps you won't mind that it's not exactly stylish at the moment. I don't believe San Francisco is going to be fashion-conscious for a few months. Except of course for earthquake fashions."

While Mama opened the package Mrs. Forrest had brought, Melora and her sister went into the hall to have a look at the trunk. Melora got her key and unlocked it and took a few things from the top tray and shook them out. She had the feeling that these garments were from another time, another world. She could remember the carefree circumstances under which she had worn this sheer waist, or that yellow voile frock with the dust ruffles and taffeta underskirt. Such froth was hardly useful at the moment, but Cora touched the bright material with wistful fingers.

"You take them," Melora said, thrusting shirtwaist and yellow frock into Cora's hands. "I've a blue serge skirt here too that will be more practical for you, but you'll want something pretty as well."

Cora caught up the garments with pleasure, and when the front door opened she held the yellow frock before her, curtseying as Tony came in with Quent behind him.

"I'm sorry," she said, "but this waltz is taken. I've promised it to—"

"To no one but me," said Tony, catching the spirit of the moment. He swung her the length of the wide polished hall, while she laughed and struggled to keep the dress from slipping.

Quent cocked an amused eyebrow at Melora and peered past her at the contents of the trunk.

"Looks like treasure trove," he said. "How about sharing with the refugees? They're asking at all the relief centers for whatever clothes can be spared."

Melora was surprised. The Quent she knew would have been quick to rise to such nonsense.

"I'll see what I can manage," she told him. "Don't forget that we have several refugees right under this roof."

Tony was whirling a breathless Cora down the hall.

Watching them, Melora felt suddenly cross and scratchy.

"I want to talk to you," she whispered to Quent.

"Well, go ahead and talk," he said, and seated himself on the rounded top of the trunk. "Hope you don't mind if I sit down. We've had quite a day. Join me?" He patted the trunk beside him.

"We can't talk here," she told him impatiently. "Quent, I really must see you alone."

He reached for her hand before she could snatch it away.

"Darling! Of course we must have some time together. I've hated to be away from you all day long."

She knew Tony heard, though he did not look around, and she snatched her hand away, wishing she were young enough to be unladylike and give Quent a good slap.

He only grinned at her glare. "Would you like to go out in the garden, dearest? Perhaps we could have a few tender words before Sam serves the spaghetti."

She certainly didn't want to go off with him on what Tony could think was a tête-à-tête.

"No thank you," she said in tones so undulcet that Cora heard, glancing at her startled. Melora went on hastily, trying to cover her sharpness. "What I'd really like is for you two boys to carry this trunk upstairs to my room. Then we could sort things out more comfortably."

Quent said, "After my day of hard labor I couldn't lift a peanut," and yawned widely.

But Tony came to take hold of one handle and tilted the trunk upward so that Quent slid from his perch. Sighing elaborately, Quent picked up his own end. He groaned all the way to the third floor, reducing Cora to helpless mirth.

Melora ran ahead to fling open her door, and the boys brought the trunk in and set it down by a window where she could get the best light for her task. As he turned to leave Tony saw the Kwan Yin. He paused beside the shelf and looked up into the golden face.

"So you found a place for her?" he said.

"You mean you lugged that all the way over here?" Quent was incredulous. "When you knew you'd need food and clothes?"

"It must be a pretty valuable piece," Tony said.

Quent shrugged. "I suppose that's different. I had to save Father's paintings because they're like cash in the bank. But, Melora, I must say I never could figure out the lady's blue hair. I remember when your father brought the statue home. I must have been about ten and I was fascinated. I've wanted to meet a lady with blue hair ever since."

Cora shooed at both boys "Skidoo now. I want to see what I can find in Mellie's trunk. I'm going to dress up for dinner."

The two girls unpacked the trunk, and Melora assigned each article to a separate pile. One for Gran, one for Cora, one for herself. A fourth pile she labeled "refugee." Some of these things might help a little.

She was happy to come upon her diary in the depths of the trunk and took it out to place beside the pile of books she was reading. As soon as she had a chance, she must start filling these pages with all the missed episodes. But there would be no time to begin before dinner.

Since there was plenty of spaghetti, Mrs. Forrest and her son had been invited to stay and they all sat around the table for dinner that night. Mr. Howard Forrest had graying hair and a young, alive look about him. He smiled at Melora and held out a hand to congratulate Quent on their engagement.

Quent was as maddening as usual. Even in his

clowning he put his finger on the one thing that left Melora helpless.

"I'm not sure but what the young lady means to call it off at any moment, sir," he said with exaggerated dolefulness. "You know how it is these days—I've a fine old family, but we're probably penniless. And who wants a penniless heir?"

Across the table Uncle Will shook his head. "My son must have his jest, Mr. Forrest. Melora will have something to say about this, I fancy."

Mama had choked over a hot forkful of Mrs. Ellis's spaghetti. She recovered herself and frowned at Quent.

"What a silly boy! To talk about the Seymours being penniless. Or about Melora throwing you over. Mr. Forrest, don't pay any attention to him."

"Quent wasn't joking about the penniless Seymours," Uncle Will said more gravely. "I've been hearing rumors about town concerning some of the insurance companies hedging on payments by invoking the earthquake clause. Of course paying up may wipe some of us out completely. But I hope to see the Seymour Company stand by every penny of its debts, whether there is anything left afterwards or not."

Mrs. Cranby turned shocked eyes upon him, but he did not seem to notice.

"This morning," he went on, "the wreckage had cooled enough so that we could dig that desk of mine out of the basement excavation pit in which it had been buried by falling debris. The thing that is giving every business the most concern just now is the complete loss of all records. Fortunately, the desk survived its ordeal and we found a batch of correspondence in it which furnishes us with some names and addresses. Also a few invaluable memorandum books. At least I have something with which to start again."

"You'll do it too," Gran said. "Addy, I've just told

Will that he can use the drawing room of this house for office purposes if he likes."

Mama choked again, but Gran went right on.

"A good many residences are going to find themselves turned part office for a while until we've rebuilt our downtown area. We might as well help to meet the need."

Mr. Forrest nodded. "The way Fillmore and Van Ness are bursting out as business sections, I'm wondering if Market Street may not have brand new rivals. Incidentally, Mrs. Bonner, if there's any possibility of your putting Mother and me up tonight as paying guests, we'd like to take advantage of it. I am most interested in—"

"Oh, not as paying guests!" cried Mama faintly.

"Addy," Gran said, "we might as well face the fact that all the rules changed at 5:14 last Wednesday morning with the earthquake. We'll be glad to have you stay of course, Mr. Forrest—you and Nell. For the moment at least this house is in business and we'll need paying guests."

Mr. Forrest's eyes twinkled. "The reason I'm interested in staying another day is because as soon as we can start printing the magazine again I'll want to run several articles about every aspect of the earthquake and fire. The whole country will want to know the truth about what has happened. And even more, it will want to know what San Francisco is going to do about it. Mother has agreed to run around tomorrow and play reporter, while I try to cover different ground. The big story, it seems to me, is about the way the city is pitching in with a will to recover. I've never seen anything like it."

There was a silence while Sam padded in with more spaghetti and Melora found herself musing aloud.

"I wish there was some way I could pitch in. I don't

want to sit home while everyone else is out working, but where can I start?"

"It isn't necessary for young ladies to—" Mama began, but Quent gave her a smile of apology and broke in.

"You bet your life you can do something, Melora! Just let me take you over to one of the relief centers tomorrow morning. They'll work you till you drop." He turned to Mrs. Cranby to forestall her objections. "They need more help and need it badly. Aunt Addy, you'll be doing the town a service if you let her go."

"Well," said Mama, "since she'll be in your care, Quentin. . . . Perhaps it will be all right for a day."

"She won't be in my care," Quent said. "Father's car's in Red Cross service now and I'm driving it. But I can take her out and bring her home."

"I'll be ready," Melora told him, smiling reassuringly at her mother. This was a chance she didn't mean to let slip.

Of course Cora wanted to go too, but Mama was firm. Cora was too young. And she had not the freedom of an engaged girl.

When the matter had been settled, Mr. Forrest began to query Mrs. Ellis about her relatives on Telegraph Hill. She talked readily, drawing a vivid picture of the way crowds had swarmed to the clearing at the top of the hill. And of how Antonio and Vito Lombardi had joined with neighbors in saving a cluster of houses that clung to the cliffside.

Tony stared uncomfortably at his plate and Melora had the feeling that for some reason he disapproved.

11

BREAD LINE

The next morning, when Quent and Melora set out, Mrs. Forrest decided to go along in order to get a glimpse of what was happening.

The relief station to which Quent was taking Melora was down in the Mission district, on the edge of the burned section. An old shed had been put to use and as they drew near Melora saw that mountains of bread and pyramids of canned milk had been piled on long boards supported by trestles. Men and women, and even a sprinkling of children, stood in a line that stretched down the block, and would be much longer before the day was over.

While Mrs. Forrest waited in the car, Quent took Melora into a tent where a bedraggled woman sat on a camp stool staring with disapproval at her own feet. Mrs. Dunlap acknowledged Quent's introduction and said she could use another pair of hands—and especially feet.

"I ought to work in my stocking feet today," she said. "The only pair of shoes I have don't fit and my feet killed me all day yesterday."

Quent told Melora he'd be back for her at the end of the day. "Don't work too hard," he said and grinned as he went off.

Mrs. Dunlap squeezed her feet back into shoes and stood up. Obviously, as a lady, she could not go out to her station shoeless, any more than she could go hatless. She straightened her befeathered hat and shook out her heavy wine-red skirt. The hem of the skirt was decidedly the worse for wear and there were rents in one or two places.

"Sometimes," she said, "I am tempted to cut my skirts off right up to the ankle. It's ridiculous to drag all this through ashes and brick dust in order to get around. Well, my dear, we're glad to have you. Come along and we'll get started. So far we haven't received nearly enough bread, but I'm sure San Francisco is flooded with enough condensed milk to last for the next ten years. And no soap! No one seems to have thought of sending in a single cake of soap. Here you are, my dear."

At first as Melora checked bread cards and reached for loaf after loaf to put into waiting hands, the faces of those in line had individuality for her. She saw the old and the young, the poor and the recently rich, the cheerful and the sad. The hands that reached toward her were sometimes gnarled and blue-veined, sometimes plump and beringed; sometimes they were the hands of a workman, or a school girl, or the small hands of a child. More often than not there was a thank-you and a smile. There was even the atmosphere of a picnic about the whole affair. But as the day wore on lines grew longer. Those who waited grew tired and those who doled out the supplies wearied even more.

At lunch time, when Melora sat down to eat the sandwich she had brought, her feet ached and her smile had turned to cardboard. By afternoon more mountains of bread came in, so there was no need to turn the crowds away. There were more relief workers too, both men and women, but Melora began to feel sure that all San Francisco had chosen to come to this one station. Faces blurred into a featureless stream. She moved automatically and would have handed Quent a loaf of bread when he turned up at her side if he hadn't taken it out of her hands and drawn her away from her place behind board and trestle.

"They're closing down now," he said. "I've come to take you home."

She walked wordlessly to where the Oldsmobile stood beside the curb, a Red Cross displayed on its side.

"Good for you for sticking it out," he went on as he helped her into the front seat. "You'll be all right as soon as you've had time to relax and get your breath."

Melora sank back in the leather seat, while Quent cranked the machine and sprang up behind the wheel.

"So many, many people who have lost everything," she said dazedly. "Even walking among the ruins I didn't realize. And they're all so ready to start over. You hardly ever hear a complaint."

"I know," Quent said. "This whole week I've been practically bursting with pride because I'm a San Franciscan." Then he looked sheepish. "Don't mind my lapse into the sentimental—it's temporary."

If she hadn't been so tired she might have answered. She'd liked him better for his show of feeling.

After that they were silent. The wind was blowing in from the Gate and Melora was grateful for the chill of it against her face. She had no motoring veil over her sailor hat and strands of hair whipped out from the restraint of bone hairpins. No matter. She couldn't care less.

Vaguely she recalled that she had wanted to talk to Quent alone. But she could not rouse herself to make the effort.

They had covered four blocks when the engine

wheezed and died. Quent tried cranking again, but nothing happened. He sighed ruefully.

"Sometimes I think Father is right and the automobile will never replace the horse. Well, there's nothing for it. I'll have to take a look at the critter's innards. Why don't you curl up in the back seat, Melora, and see if you can catch forty winks while I tinker?"

She caught more than forty winks, for it took Quent a while to find the difficulty. She went soundly asleep and only wakened when a terrible dream of earthquake and roaring fire engulfed her and jarred her back to consciousness. She sat up in the back seat to find the car vibrating, the engine sputtering and blasting.

Quent got the car into motion before it changed its mind. As she shook the heaviness of sleep from her eyes, Melora felt refreshed and rested. Her feet had stopped throbbing.

This time the car made it clear up the hill to Lafayette Square—almost home—before one of the tires gave out with a long wheezing sigh as the air whistled out of it.

Quent looked over his shoulder at Melora. "As I was saying about horses— Well, never mind. Let's leave the car here for now and walk across the park. I'll come back and change the tire tonight or tomorrow morning. I've had enough for the moment."

He opened the rear door and held out his hand as she stepped down. Fog was drifting in overhead and in the park the refugees crawled into tents and shelters, or pulled what wraps they had about them. The sight was so familiar now that Melora hardly gave them a second look. She was awake, her mind alert. Now she could choose the words she must speak to Quent.

"I want to give you back your ring," she said, slipping it from her finger as they walked along. "I don't think this was very clever of us in the first place. And now it seems merely childish. The only thing to do is tell everyone the truth and stop this silly pretense."

"I haven't noticed you pretending very hard," Quent said. He kept his hands in his pockets and did not even look at the ring she held out to him. His mouth had tightened as if he were angry.

"Let's not argue about it," Melora said. "I don't want to be burdened with this any longer."

"Because of Tony?"

She hated the warmth that swept into her cheeks. "Of course not! Tony hasn't anything to do with it. I hardly know him and—"

"Spare me the denials," he said. "I'm not blind, even if your mother is." He turned on the path and faced her. "Look, Melora, I've known you most of my life. And I know Tony pretty well. I know he's all wrong for you."

Now it was her turn to grow angry. "Tony regards you as a friend," she said coldly. "But I can't say you're proving yourself a very loyal one. Besides, why should you care what I think of Tony?"

For a moment he didn't answer, then he spoke as coldly as she. "You're quite right, Melora. It's nothing to me what you do." He started on again and she walked beside him. "But the others concerned do mean something to me. This is no time to upset everybody with our foolishness. Whether you and I are engaged or not engaged, isn't anything to carry on about at this particular time. Your mother has enough to worry her. Though it's really Father I'm thinking of most. I hadn't dreamed he'd be so pleased. Now, with all he has on his shoulders, I'd feel guilty about disillusioning him."

"I'm not happy about having fooled him either," Melora admitted, "but just the same I don't want to—"

Quent cut her off. "Father's putting up a good front,

but he's worried sick about what's going to happen. He doesn't see any way out at the moment. He has already written Mother telling her to stay in New York with our eastern relatives for now. But she'll have to take Gwen out of private school when the term is up."

"I—I'm sorry about that," Melora said helplessly.

They had reached the downhill path and they stood for a moment side by side while Melora balanced the ring in her hand. She didn't want to return it to her finger, yet she felt trapped by Quent's words, just as she had been by Gran's. It wasn't just that she didn't want people to think ill of her. She couldn't humiliate Uncle Will like this, or have Quent's pride hurt by the remarks others might make about the broken engagement.

"Put it on," Quent said more gently. "Even if it doesn't mean anything, I'm trusting you with it. Some day I may want it for something that isn't make-believe. You'd better not lose it."

She slipped it back on her finger and started downhill. "All right then. We'll leave it this way for now."

"Good enough," Quent said, but he sounded stiff and distant.

They walked the rest of the way home in silence.

12

———◆———

STEPS
TO NOWHERE

Many things happened early in May. A warming, reassuring letter arrived from Melora's father. The one thing he cared about, he wrote, was to know they were all safe. The loss of possessions did not really matter. He loved them all and he would be with them before very long.

Mama and Cora wept openly over the letter. Melora's eyes were wet too. When her father came home everything would be made right. It had always been so.

There was a letter from Quent's mother also. She wrote in a more excited vein, both anguished and despairing. Sylvia Seymour was not one to shrug possessions aside so lightly. Uncle Will read parts of her letter to them at dinner one evening and shook his head over it worriedly.

He was going through a difficult period and Quent had had to stop driving for the Red Cross and stay home to assist him. The moment the location of the temporary Seymour office had been made public through the newspapers, lines of policy holders had

120

begun to form outside the Bonner house. People who held policies with the company, but who had, most of them, lost all their own records and papers, were now demanding that Seymour's pay up the insurance at once and in full. This of course was impossible. Even if the company had been prepared to meet so heavy a load of payments, money was still the scarcest commodity in the city and though the banks were open again, withdrawals had been limited to five hundred dollars per depositor.

Day after day Quent and his father and one or two clerks had interviewed the endless lines of men and women who had insurance with the company.

A number of good things had happened too, however. Glass, shattered by the quake, was now back in the windows, so the house was warmer. There was plenty of water again and an inspector had come around to look at repaired chimneys and had given out permits to build fires indoors. The gas and electricity were still off, though there were no longer any limitations on using lamps and candles at night.

The Hooper family, who had rented this house from Grandmother, returned and announced that they had had enough of San Francisco. They were newly settled in Oakland. Mrs. Hooper sent a dray for their belongings. There was still enough of the original Bonner furniture to keep the house going. And the money paid in by the "boarders" had helped to buy new supplies, now available in the stores again.

One-story redwood shops were going up on Van Ness Avenue, and some of San Francisco's best stores were opening for business. Fillmore was crowded with stores and offices, flags flying everywhere, with what Gran said was a regular mining town atmosphere.

There had been one change among the boarders.

Mrs. Ellis had gone to live with her family on Telegraph Hill, though Tony had remained. Transportation was still a problem and he was nearer to the new Gower & Ellis shop here.

Mr. Gower had located in an old house on Van Ness and was stocking it with books he managed to obtain on credit. Mama had shaken her head over such optimism. Who could afford books at a time when even potatoes were a luxury? But Gran said if she knew the human species, this would be the very time when people would reach out for luxuries. And indeed, Tony reported that buyers were coming in. He said too that in the makeshift shops people were buying silks and satins, as often as they bought workaday materials. Insurance money had begun to come in from outside companies and people who had seldom had money to spend before, now found themselves with cash in pocket. The prospect of more was always good for credit.

Melora continued with her work at the relief center until she was no longer needed. Still unfinished in the drawer of the table in her room was the detailed account she had started to write her father about the days of the fire. She'd had no time to work on it further. Instead, she had written him a more hurried letter, and had almost forgotten the other.

She was sitting in her room that afternoon in late May writing in her diary, glancing up now and then to look out the window toward the Gate. For once no fog was rolling in and the sun was bright as it dipped toward the water. Watching the sails of vessels standing out clearly against it, she recalled something Tony had told her recently when they were talking about books. It was something he had read. The Costanoans, who had been natives of California before the Spaniards came, had called the Pacific the Sundown Sea.

A lovely name. She could remember the way Tony had spoken the words, giving them a ringing sound. Only Tony, of all the people she knew, seemed to realize that words in themselves could move the emotions, stir the imagination. Perhaps that was because he wanted to be an actor. He liked to roll words sonorously on his tongue, so that it was thrilling to hear him recite poetry.

Tony, Tony, Tony.

She found she was writing his name on the diary page before her and threw down her pen. Did he think of her too like this? But how could she ever know as long as Quent's ring stood guard upon her finger?

Her mother's voice calling from the stairs broke in upon her thoughts. "Melora! Have you seen Alec? Is he with you?"

Melora roused herself and went to the door. Right after lunch, she told her mother, she had heard Alec say that he was going out to play with his friends in the square.

Mama wrung her hands despairingly. "That riffraff! Refugees! Do come help us look for him, Melora. We can't find him anywhere."

"We're refugees too," Melora couldn't help reminding her. "We're just the lucky ones with a roof over our heads."

But it was true Alec had begun to run with a gang of rather rough boys older than he was. She knew her mother's concern might well be justified.

"Quong Sam has gone over to the square," Gran said when they came downstairs. "He knows which boys Alec plays with and where their families are. He'll bring the boy home, so stop fussing, Addy."

It was nearing suppertime. Tony had just come

home, and Quent, hearing excited voices, had left the drawing-room-office where he was helping his father finish up the day's work. In a few minutes Sam was back, having collared two boys of ten and eleven. He marched the two firmly to the foot of the steps.

"You talkee!" he said when he had confronted them with Mama, who hurried out to the little balcony above the steps. "You tellee Missy Clanby whassa matta Alec."

The two boys looked plainly frightened, but they stopped their wriggling and the younger one began to blubber.

"We tol' him and tol' him not to tag around after us! We don't wanta play with babies all the time!"

Gran came to the top of the steps looking down at them. "Where did you go today when Alec tagged after you?" she asked sternly.

The older boy wriggled under Sam's firm grip. "Gosh, your Chinaman is choking me! What Billy says is right. Some of us wanted to go exploring up on Nob Hill and we told him he was too little and he should ought to stay home. But he come along anyway. We didn't tell him to do what he did."

"Never mind that!" said Gran. "What did he do?"

"Well—he knew we thought he was a baby and he got this notion he could show us he was just as brave as us. So there was this burned-down house with the big high steps and he said—that is, we said we bet he couldn't go up there and jump off the top down into the ruins."

Mama cried out at that. "There was another quake this afternoon!"

"What happened, fellow?" Quent broke in. "Hurry up and tell us."

The boy went on, his words dragging. "Alec climbed up those ol' steps all right. And his dog went up 'em too. We—we just left him there and came home."

"It was a good chance to get away from him," the smaller boy put in. "Honest, ma'am, we didn't try to make him jump."

"Did he, or didn't he?" Gran snapped.

Both boys shook their heads. "We don't know, ma'am," the older boy said. "We didn't stay to see. We just thought he'd come on down and go home himself when he found we'd beat it."

"Where is this house with the steps?" Quent asked.

The older boy said, "Up near the top of the hill somewhere. It's hard to tell where places are any more."

"Think you could find your way back and show us the steps?" Quent asked.

"My mom said I was to come right home to our tent and not go any place else," the younger boy put in promptly.

Matt, the older one, however, was willing to try.

Quent reassured Mrs. Cranby and Gran. "Don't worry. I'll hitch up the rig and take this fellow up Nob Hill right away. We'll find Alec all right."

"I know he's been hurt!" Mama cried. "I can feel it. If he could have come home he'd have been here long before this. Do hurry, Quent."

Melora followed Quent down to the carriage house at the foot of the garden and Tony came with her.

"Let me go along, Quent," Melora offered. "Maybe I can help if—if Alec really is hurt."

Quent nodded, wasting no time as he busied himself with Dolly, the mare. Tony helped too, and Melora recognized that he had made himself one of the rescue party.

The boy Matt was no longer interested in escape, but was now eager to help with Alec's rescue. A thin, wiry boy, he squeezed himself on the floor against the dash at their feet, leaving the seat for them.

The constant noises of dismantling and rebuilding were a part of everyday existence now. The ring of the hammer could be heard day and night, even from Lafayette Square, and as the buggy crossed Van Ness and started up the hill, the din increased. Dolly had grown used to the racket and hardly twitched an ear, but the grotesque angles of the ruins still worried her and she had a tendency to shy. Now and then she snorted furiously as if the very smell offended her.

As they plodded up Nob Hill the racket lessened and the streets were deserted again. The nabobs of Nob Hill were not returning to build anew with quite the speed of the rest of the city. Only on the Fairmont Hotel had rebuilding begun.

Matt craned this way and that, trying to recall the zigzag trail his gang had followed early that afternoon.

"Seems to me this place had a big garden at the side," he recalled. "The fence was all twisted and I think that's the place where some of the kids shied rocks at statues. There was a statue of a lady holding a bow, only her head was cracked off."

"Diana," Quent said, flapping the reins over Dolly's back. "I think I know the place you mean."

But even knowing it didn't make its discovery any too easy, thanks to the wrecking of most familiar landmarks. The rose and purple ruins all about bore little resemblance to the mansions which had once graced Nob Hill.

"From now on," Tony said, "I think every nightmare I have will be haunted by piles of brick. Did you ever see so many bricks in all your life?" He straightened in the seat. "Look, Quent! Along the hill there—is that our headless Diana?"

Quent nodded. "That's the place I was thinking of."

The once beautiful garden with its ordered flower beds was a bare expanse of burned and blackened stubble. Mosaic tile marked the remains of a fountain and Diana stood headless on her pedestal, poised on one toe, a bow in her broken hands.

Up the hill beyond the garden rose a steep flight of steps leading nowhere. A single stark chimney was all that remained of the sumptuous house.

"That's the place all right!" Matt cried. He wriggled out from under their feet and swung down from the buggy.

"Wait, Matt," Melora said quickly. "Those steps may not be safe."

Tony came with her, while Quent secured Dolly. They started cautiously up the flight of steps. The rail was twisted and bent outward, the bricks along the outer edge had crumbled, offering no support to a careless foot. As usual when the wind blew over the hill a fine white dust stirred above the ruins.

The steps jogged upward, turning at right angles in two places. If one kept to the center they looked safe enough and Melora picked up her fraying gray skirt and climbed to the first landing, with the others right behind her. From above a sudden yelping and whining greeted her and Smokey came dashing frantically down the steps toward them.

Melora caught him in her arms and let him lick at her face in excitement. There was no doubt now that this was the right place and that Alec was somewhere nearby. At the top landing Melora put the little dog down and looked over the drop into space beyond. Here everything had crashed through into the cellar and there was indeed a jumping-off space such as Matt had described.

"This is right," Matt said. "He—he said he wasn't afraid to jump off here."

Melora shivered as she looked down into the piles of brick and masonry, of every sort of rubble. Nothing moved. There was so sign of any living creature.

"Alec!" she called. "Alec, where are you?"

Hollow walls on the hillside threw back the echo mockingly, but no boy's voice answered her call.

Quent looked over too, bending to stroke Smokey's head and quiet him. "A jump wouldn't be too bad. That's loose stuff down there, and if he landed on the stone ledge that broken pillar makes, he'd be all right. It could be that he's down there exploring."

"Don't forget that quake this afternoon," Tony reminded them.

Quent turned to Matt, shaking him by the collar. "Where were you boys when the quake came this afternoon?"

Matt squirmed under his grip. "Leggo! Lemme think. I guess we were part way home by that time. Yeah—we'd just got to Van Ness, because I remember we ran out into the middle of the street in spite of all the wagons and things."

"Then Alec might have been down there at the time." Melora turned to Quent. "What can we do?"

Quent cupped his hands about his mouth and shouted Alec's name. His voice was stronger than Melora's and it sent the echoes crashing.

"There!" Tony cried, pointing. "Way at the back. Something moved."

Melora saw it too—an arm in a dark sleeve, waving weakly. "It's Alec!" she cried. "Listen!"

The faintest of calls came to them; a thin "Help me!"

Quent moved first. "We can get through by way

of the garden and reach him. Melora, you stay here and—"

But she was already running down the steps behind him.

Quent and Matt hurried ahead and Tony took her arm lest she stumble as they ran across the ruined garden. Smokey, wild with excitement, seemed to be under all their heels at once.

At the rear of the cellar there were no walls, but only one tall chimney which looked solid enough. Melora slipped and stumbled over loose bricks and broken stone, grateful for Tony's hand. Quent always left her to fend for herself. She had done so since they were children. She was comforted by Tony's thoughtfulness.

She could see Alec now, lying face down in the rubble, his eyes closed, his face white except for a streaking of blood on his forehead. Except for his head and shoulders, he lay completely buried, pinned amid the wreckage.

She knelt on the bricks beside him, scarcely feeling the sharpness as they cut into her knees and scraped the skin of her hands.

"Alec!" Her voice was faint because of the fear that shook her. He was so dreadfully quiet. But as she spoke his name, he opened his eyes and turned his head a little so he could look up at her. Smokey was whining about him, sniffing and nuzzling.

"I knew you'd come, Mellie." Alec's voice was weak but clear. "I told Smokey to go get you." He saw Matt then, standing miserably by. "I jumped, but you didn't stay to see. I jumped all the way."

"I know," Matt spoke with a choke in his voice.

Alec only said, "Pull me out, Mellie. It—hurts."

Quent and Tony were wasting no time on talk. With their bare hands they were trying to dig away the rubble, but the hopelessness of the task was evident at once. Some of the bigger pieces were wedged and there was too much to be moved by the slow hand process. Quent straightened and spoke to Tony.

"You stay with Melora and Alec. I'm going to take the buggy and go down where I can get some workmen with shovels, somebody to help. I'll make it fast." He bent over Alec. "You'll be all right, fellow. Just you hold on a while longer."

Alec tried to nod, but only moaned faintly.

When Matt went off with Quent, Melora quickly cleared a place near Alec so she could sit close to him and rest his head against her thigh.

"Mellie," he said, "will they hurry? Will it take them very long?"

She wiped the perspiration from his face with her handkerchief. "I'm sure it won't. They'll be back in a jiffy to get you out of here."

"Tell me a story, Mellie," he whispered. "Maybe they'll come faster if you tell me a story."

She tried to remember one of his favorite King Arthur stories, or a scene from *Treasure Island*— anything at all. But she was too upset to concentrate. The words came haltingly and she looked at Tony for help.

He sat on a pile of brick on the other side of Alec, with Smokey at his feet. There was nothing flashing and dramatic about him now. His eyes were dark with sympathy, but he managed a smile.

"Suppose I tell you a story," he said.

13

SIXTH SON

While Melora stroked Alec's forehead with gentle fingers, and rubbed the back of his neck, helping him to relax, Tony began his story. Melora hardly listened. What would they find when that heap of rubble was cleared away? How badly had he been crushed? Any movement caused him pain, and fear was a hard, tight ball inside her.

But as Tony's quiet voice went on, somehow compelling, Melora began to hear the words and realize that it was a true story he was telling.

It had begun many years before, when two young men had gone into partnership in the opening of a small bookstore in San Francisco. The city had always been a book-conscious town and the two young partners did well. Both earnestly loved good books, but they were not alike. One was more a businessman, practical and unromantic, preferring to read heavy tomes of philosophy and science. The younger man was as romantic as the stories he liked to read, and he was always dreaming himself into the role of hero in stories he made up. He even thought of putting those stories down on paper some day, but he never seemed to get around to it, though he had had a slim volume of poetry published.

This younger partner had a second love besides books—he was a devotee of music and especially of the opera. He could not afford expensive seats, but he missed no opera which played the city.

One afternoon, well on toward closing time, when his partner was in the back of the store totaling up the day's receipts, a young woman walked in looking for a particular book on music.

"How many times I've heard my father describe just the way she looked when she came in that day," Tony said.

"You mean the younger partner was your own father?" Alec asked, and Melora could have blessed Tony for catching his interest.

"That's right. And he said Lotta Lombardi was the most beautiful girl he had ever seen. She had shining dark eyes that could be kind one moment and angry the next. She wore her masses of black hair in a heavy coil on her neck, with a little tilted hat tipping toward her nose. Her perfume seemed as lovely and mysterious as the girl herself, and her smile did queer things to his heart. Of course he knew who she was the moment he saw her."

Tony paused dramatically and Melora glanced at him. He was plainly lost in his own story.

"Go on!" Alec demanded. "Who was she?"

The young man, Tony explained, had heard her sing in the opera the night before. Not that she sang a star's role—only a small bit. But her voice and the fire with which she performed had impressed the critics and she had been acclaimed in her role in the papers that very morning. So of course she was pleased and elated when this unknown young man in the bookstore confessed that he had heard her sing, remembered her well, and agreed with the critics.

It was a slow, rainy afternoon and no other customers came into the shop. When it was closing time, he simply fastened the bolt across the door and went right on with the discussion he was having with the lovely singer. They were by that time arguing the virtues and faults of a new opera which had lately played the city. Miss Lotta Lombardi sat upon a ledge with book shelves rising above her head and sang snatches of arias to prove her point.

"And do you know what she proved?" Tony asked.

"What?" demanded Alec, caught up in the illusion of Tony's story.

"She proved, of course," said Tony, "that she was the one girl in the world whom my father intended to marry."

"And he *did* marry her!" Alec cried. "She's your mother!"

Tony nodded and then turned his head, listening. "I thought I heard a horse's hooves. But perhaps I was wrong. Listen to that wind."

It was rising now and it made an eerie sound whistling around chimneys and broken walls, blowing through windows that opened on nothing.

"Tell me another story," Alec pleaded.

"All right," Tony said, "listen to this one. Once upon a time many years after that day when Lotta Lombardi walked into the bookshop and caused my father to fall in love with her, another young man worked in that very same shop. And one day he too saw a young lady walk in. But this young lady was carefully guarded by her mother. Though she came with some frequency and he always watched her, it was difficult to speak to her alone. Until one day when he used a little trickery so that he could have a few moments to talk to her."

"And did that young man marry the girl too?" asked Alec.

Tony laughed and Melora looked away. "You're

going a bit too fast now, young fellow. This time our hero had the misfortune to discover that the young lady who interested him so much was engaged to someone else."

Melora was conscious of the sparkle of the heirloom diamond on her left hand. She spoke without raising her eyes.

"Why did this young lady interest him?"

Tony was silent and she knew she had surprised him with the sudden question, even as she had surprised herself. But with the spell of that other story upon her, and the restraint of Quent's ring on her finger, she'd had to ask it.

Alec moved restlessly. Smokey jumped up and began to bark loudly.

"Here they come!" cried Tony. "Hush, boy. These are friends." Then his eyes met Melora's steadily. "If you'd like to know, I'll tell you sometime just what he saw."

Quent and the three men he'd brought back were there with shovels, and they all fell to work. Melora remained where she was with Alec's head against her leg. She closed her eyes, afraid to watch. She could feel Alec quiver and she winced at the sounds of rubble being tossed aside. She didn't look until she heard Quent's exclamation of relief.

"What luck! These two big stones seemed to have wedged together and held the full weight of the stuff away from him. But I think his leg is caught in the wedge. Easy now, Alec."

Alec cried out just once as they freed him, and then Melora had him in her arms. He was too heavy to lift and Quent took him from her. Alec's right leg dangled at a sickening angle, but whether he was otherwise hurt would take a doctor to tell. They carried him to the buggy as quickly as they could.

Alec's face was screwed up with pain, but he had

seen Matt and he would not cry out again. One of the workmen said he was going toward Lafayette Square and would see that Matt got home, so they needn't be crowded. Quent took up the reins and Melora held Alec in her lap, with his hurt leg across Tony's knees. Smokey crouched at their feet, looking up now and then to reassure himself that his master was still there.

The sun had gone down and the opal twilight was fading. A big moon, just risen, hung low in the sky, giving a metallic glow to ruin and desolation. As the buggy jogged toward the dip of the hill, the pale light touched a shimmering white doorway that rose below them. A half dozen marble pillars, classically beautiful, supported the marble beam of a door. Three shallow marble steps led upward between the pillars. There was nothing more—just that ghostly doorway, the darkening sky beyond, and through the opening, silhouetted against the sky, the faraway, shattered dome of City Hall.

"Look!" cried Melora softly. "How lonely it seems!"

"That's where the Townes lived," Quent said. "Looks like everything's gone except the marble doorway."

"Doorway into the past," said Tony softly.

The buggy turned the corner and jogged on.

"Depends on which way you look through it," Quent said. "Maybe it's a doorway to the future."

To cheer Alec he began to sing and the other two joined in.

> Merrily we roll along, roll along, roll aong;
> Merrily we roll along o'er the deep blue sea.

But even while Melora's lips moved in the words, she found that her thoughts were divided. Alec's hurt first, and her worry about how serious it was. Then Tony's words back there in the ruins—when he might have told her what he saw in that girl who came into the shop with her mother. And finally, the queer thing that Quent had said just now about the marble doorway. Not a door into the past, as Tony had called it, but one to the future. She would never have expected Quent to say a thing like that.

At home there was a commotion when the boys carried Alec in, but surprisingly Mama did not go all to pieces. It was as if she had reached the very pit of despair when she thought Alec had been killed. Nothing else could ever be as bad as that.

Watching her, Melora remembered how Gran had said they'd have to give her a little time.

Quong Sam had gone for a doctor. Cora was setting water to heat in the kitchen, and Quent and Tony had been shooed out of the way by Gran. Since there was nothing more Melora could do at the moment, she went upstairs to her room.

Pulling open the small drawer of her table, she took out the sheets of paper on which she had started that account for her father so many days ago. The urge to write to him was strong now—her diary wouldn't do. But somehow the words came too fast and in too disordered a fashion to make sense. There seemed to be altogether too much to tell all at once.

While she sat there, helpless to make her pencil do her bidding, she heard someone knocking downstairs at the front door. Everyone else was busy, so she went down to answer it.

The man who stood at the door was Chinese, though he wore no queue down his back. He was rather a young man, dressed not as an Oriental servant, but in a conservative American business suit of dark gray. He bowed ceremoniously and spoke without a trace of pidgin English.

"Good evening. I am sorry to trouble you, but is this the house of Mrs. Bonner?"

"That's right," Melora said.

"I am looking for my uncle, Quong Sam," the young man went on. "After the recent disaster he sent word to me in Berkeley, but I have been concerned for him. I decided to come over and see for myself. My name is Eddie Quong."

"We're happy to see you," she said. "I'm Melora Cranby. Please come in." As she led him into the parlor she went on to explain. "Quong Sam is out just now—getting a doctor. My young brother has had an accident. But he'll be back soon and you'll find him in good health. He's been wonderful. I don't know what we'd have done without him. Won't you sit down?"

Young Mr. Quong said he regretted to hear of her brother's accident. He hesitated just a moment before he seated himself in a parlor chair. "I am not sure my uncle will approve if he finds me here." He smiled faintly.

"I don't know why not," said Melora. "Sam is one of the family, goodness knows. We're happy to welcome any relative of his."

Gran had heard the knocking and she came downstairs to see who was there. When Melora introduced Eddie Quong, she held out her hand in warm greeting.

"I overheard what my granddaughter just told you," she said, "and it is very true. It would be hard to imagine this household without your uncle. But in all these years we have never once met any of his family. There's been a legend for the last twenty years at least that he was putting a nephew through an American college, so we're delighted to meet the nephew. But, young man, I'm sure you haven't been going to college for twenty years, so I'm still mystified."

Eddie Quong seemed to relax a little with Gran and lose something of his Chinese reticence. "Such matters my uncle would keep to himself. Mrs. Bonner, I am my father's sixth son. My uncle has put five older brothers of mine through school and they are now living in different parts of this country. I am the last. He will be released from a burden when I graduate."

Melora could only stare. Quong Sam living so frugally on his pay that he could do a thing like this! And they'd really known nothing about it.

"Your uncle has no other family then?" Gran asked.

Eddie Quong shook his head. "His own wife and three children died long ago in China in a smallpox epidemic. The same epidemic which marked my uncle's face. After his loss he decided to come to this country. His older brother financed his trip and he promised that in return, when he was able to earn, he would send his brother's sons through school in America, if they wished to come here."

It was an astonishing story. Too many families took the years of loyalty their Chinese servants gave for granted, knowing little about their private lives, or what their personal problems might be. This was partly due to Chinese reserve which held off outside curiosity. A family seldom dared ask personal questions of the Chinese they employed.

Before Gran could say anything more Quong Sam arrived with the doctor and took him upstairs at once. Gran called to him to come down when he was through, and his "Yes, Missy" floated back to them down the stair well.

Gran held out her hand to Eddie Quong. "If you'll excuse me, I must go upstairs. But come to see us again, Mr. Quong. We are proud to know a nephew of Quong Sam's."

The young man stood up and bowed courteously, but there was a rueful note to his words.

"Thank you, Mrs. Bonner, but my uncle would not approve."

Gran raised her eyebrows, but matters upstairs drew her and she hurried away. Melora remained with Eddie Quong and when Sam came scuttling downstairs to the parlor, she saw his disapproval. Sam had only a curt greeting. His look seemed to take in the fact that his nephew was sitting like company in the parlor of the house in which his uncle worked. Sam gestured at once toward his own cellar quarters and spoke volubly in Chinese.

Eddie Quong snapped to his feet as if a string had pulled him. His face showed no expression except for the eyes which turned once in Melora's direction, as if in apology. But it was an aplogy for himself, not for his uncle.

As Sam hurried off, not troubling to look back, Eddie Quong made Melora the same formal bow he had given Gran.

"My uncle is old China," he said softly as he turned to follow. Then, lest she misunderstand, he stopped and faced her again. "It is a very fine thing to be old China," he said and disappeared in the direction Sam had taken.

Melora went upstairs, touched by the little encounter. Sam was a darling, though there was no way of ever telling him so. And she liked the young nephew.

Cora came out of Mama's room just as she reached the door. "You can't go in," she said. "The doctor's sent me out too. He's going to set Alec's leg. I—let's not stay here." She put her hands over her ears, and together they ran up to Melora's room.

"Tell me about what happened when you went after Alec," Cora said, and Melora explained how they'd climbed the steps and found Alec in the ruins, and of how she and Tony had stayed with him while Quent went for help.

"I wish I'd been there too," Cora said.

Melora regarded her steadily. "Why do you wish that?"

"Oh, I don't know." Cora's eyes avoided her sister's. "I suppose—except that Alec was hurt—it would have been something exciting to do."

There was a little silence. Melora had picked up her pencil and was idly drawing circles on a corner of the paper which still lay on the table.

"I've been thinking of asking Mama if we could have a party, or a picnic one of these days," she said at last. "You've lost touch with all your old friends, Cora. But I'm sure we could get Celia Norman and her brother Harry. And there's Tom and his cousin Julia. And—"

Cora broke in impatiently. "I don't give a hoot about seeing Harry or Tom. They're so young and silly and dull."

"You didn't used to think so."

"Well—a person can change. Anyway, don't bother about me, Mellie." Cora jumped up and ran to the door and down the hall to her own room before anything more could be said.

Melora stared at the paper before her. She knew well enough what Cora had not put into words. After Tony, the boys they'd known in the past did seem foolish and young and a little dull.

She sat down and began to put words on paper and now, unexpectedly, they began to make sense. She could write to her father tonight, put down something of her impressions. It was a good thing the excitement about Alec had delayed supper. She could start this now.

She began with the goodness of Quong Sam and the pride and respect his nephew bore for him. These things too were part of San Francisco.

Once Gran came to her door with the news that the doctor had set Alec's leg and there seemed to be no injuries aside from bruises and abrasions. But not even the interruption of a quick supper stopped her.

What poured out in the hours she sat at her desk was the story of people, more than of events. There was Mr. Gower giving her a book for her grandmother and later opening a store in the front room of an old mansion on Van Ness. And there was Quent, forgetting his boredom to drive a Red Cross car until he had to turn his hand to helping his father in the desperate insurance business which had never interested him before.

She wrote about Gran too, facing the sort of trouble she had had to meet more than once in her life, and facing it with unflinching courage. Alec was in the picture of course—a small boy who could not be blamed for responding to the invitation of adventure and exploration inevitably held out by the ruins.

And, finally, knowing always that she postponed what she most wanted to say, she wrote about Tony selling burned books for the Earthquake Fund and doing a good job of it. Of Tony sitting on a pile of bricks, telling a romantic story to a little boy with a broken leg.

She could see him again as she wrote and the gay, lively picture he made—unconventional, a bit dashing; someone to make the pulses quicken, to fill the eye and the memory.

But she could not write about Cora. Her sister's

interest had been caught by Tony Ellis too, and that was something she did not want to think about.

When she thought she was through and had wearily put her pencil down, she had to pick it up again to set down one more line. The words Quent had spoken when he'd said it depended on which way you looked through that lonely marble doorway on the hillside; the way he had contradicted Tony and called it a doorway to the future.

She slept very soundly that night. And Kwan Yin smiled in the darkness, wise beyond mortal wisdom.

14

THE LETTER

The next day was Thursday. And Thursday was for loose ends.

Little by little the Bonner house was evolving a working routine. Monday of course was wash day, though there were at the moment not many clothes to be washed. On Tuesday the iron heated on the kitchen stove and Quong Sam made short work of the ironing. At least they had sheets and pillowcases, even if they still lacked clothes. Wednesday was for sewing and mending, and every woman busied herself with a needle. There was mending galore, and new things to be made for all of them.

Friday was for cleaning. Dust flew as the house was shaken inside out. It flew literally because these days whenever there was a wind from the east or south, dust from the ruins seeped through every crack, defeating the most watchful broom.

On Saturday Gran herself turned to baking. Not that Quong Sam couldn't make delicious pies and cakes, but there was so much extra work for him now that Gran knew he needed help. This was not a notion that Sam himself harbored. If left alone he would have shouldered all the work himself and without complaint. But Gran said baking was a form of amusement for her and she'd go into a decline again if he didn't let her do it. Quong Sam was nearly as old as Gran and he was entirely as wise. The two eyed each other with complete understanding, and Sam, having let it be known that he was not fooled, gave way and allowed her to help him.

Only Thursday was a day of no definite assignments, and Melora rather dreaded it. As long as there was so much work that she had little time to stop and draw breath, she was all right. But these days when a lapse came, restlessness followed. In spite of the monotony and the fatigue, she'd loved working at the relief centers.

But now the relief work had become less imperative and better organized. She found herself needed only now and then, so she stayed home and helped around the house. That, she supposed, was right and proper and she had no business grumbling. Yet it was hard when she saw Tony go off every morning to work in the bookshop, and Quent go out on errands for his father.

Now it was Thursday again. When she found Cora idle too, Melora took her up to the tower room and put the stack of scribbled sheets into her hands.

"A letter to Papa," she said. "Or at least a record for him. I'll give it to him when he gets home. See what you think."

Cora began to read, her mind plainly on other matters. Once she spoke without looking up and Melora knew her sister had not focused on the written words.

"You said yesterday that when Alec was hurt and Quent went for help, Tony stayed with you."

"That's right," Melora said.

Cora ran her finger along a crease in the notepaper and Melora waited. Out on the bay a foghorn had begun its hoarse bleating, even though the sky was still sunny here.

"Does Tony ever talk about me, Mellie?" Cora asked.

"I don't recall that he does," Melora said evenly.

Cora went on, smoothing the sheets on her knee. "It's the first time I've ever felt this way. I mean— I've always known before when a boy liked me. But with Tony I can't tell for sure. Oh, of course he *likes* me, but—" she looked up, "don't you go preaching at me again!"

"I won't preach, honey," Melora said. "But I don't think you should get romantic notions about Tony."

"Oh, you always think I'm too young!" Cora cried.

"I wish you'd read my letter," Melora said, and Cora, after a grimace at her sister, began to read.

This time she paid attention to the words. She read to the very end and then looked up, her eyes shining.

"You've made it as real as—as it actually was! Mellie, this isn't just a letter for Papa. It's more than that."

"What do you mean?"

"I don't know exactly. Let's show it to Tony tonight. Maybe he'll have some idea. You just don't realize how exciting this is."

Melora reached to take the sheets back, but her sister ran laughing to the door with them behind her. Showing them to Tony was nonsense, of course. Cora had no judgment. But Cora hid the sheets in her own room and refused to return them.

There was nothing to do but shrug the matter off, though Melora continued to feel uncomfortable. She would never have written so personally for outside eyes to read.

At dinner that night Tony came late to the table. When he took his place he gave her a quick look and she knew that Cora must have slipped the letter to him. She could feel herself flush and she caught Cora's eyes in pleading. She couldn't endure it if her sister blurted everything out before the others. Cora, however, said nothing, much to Melora's relief.

Alec was upstairs in bed and had spent an uncomfortable day as the beginning of his payment for running off and behaving in so reckless a fashion. Fully recovered from her fright by now, Mama was stewing a bit about her son's behavior.

"His father will have to take him in hand the minute he gets home," Mrs. Cranby said, her cheeks pink with indignation. "I can't discipline him properly any more and he must be made to stay home and mind me to the letter."

Gran looked up from ladling stew onto serving plates Sam had placed before her.

"Trouble is," Gran said, "you discipline him one minute and spoil him the next. So the poor child is mixed up most of the time. But aside from that I don't think it would be a good idea to discipline him to the point where he never did anything adventuresome or reckless again."

Mama looked shocked, but Uncle Will Seymour nodded.

"You can't mean," Mama began, "that I'm just to let him run loose—"

"Not entirely," Gran said. "Every parent is pulled between the difficulties of keeping a child alive and yet not stifling something in him that's there for the good of the human race. What sort of people would we San Franciscans be now if we had no trace of the adventurous in us? Pretty flabby, I'm sure. Alec's got something of both his father and his grandfather in him, and I think we ought to be glad of it."

"Hear, hear!" said Uncle Will before Mama could

speak. "Some of his grandmother in him too, if I'm not mistaken."

Melora glanced at Tony in time to catch his eyes upon her. He smiled faintly and she knew he had read those pages Cora had given him. But what he thought of them she could not tell.

When the meal was finished the group drifted into the parlor to talk and read the papers. Mama went upstairs to Alec, and Tony stopped Melora in the doorway.

"Come out in the garden for a moment," he said.

They went out the rear door together and down to a low stone wall between the garden and the drive.

"It's rather difficult," Tony said, when she was perched on the wall beside him, "to find a chance to speak to a young lady who is engaged. But I felt you wouldn't want to talk about this before everybody else." He took the folded sheets from an inside pocket and spread them on his knee.

"I—I expect it's pretty awful. It was ridiculous of Cora to show it to you. I didn't intend—"

"You needn't apologize," he said. "This account deserves to be published. I remember Mr. Forrest saying that the country would be eager for firsthand accounts of what had happened here in San Francisco, and of how people were facing up to it. You've presented both vividly."

"But—it's all personal," Melora protested. "I've used the names of real people. I've told things that happened to *us*."

"That's why it's convincing. But don't worry about that. The names can be changed, the details disguised. What you must do is send this quickly to *Mission Bells*. Let Mr. Forrest read it."

Melora shook her head. "Oh, I couldn't! He'd only laugh at me."

She was alarmed at his indignation. "Why do you

have so little confidence in yourself, Melora Cranby? And so little confidence in my judgment? Do you think I've never read a good piece of writing before?"

"I'm sorry," she said, humbled.

"I can understand that you might be shy about sending the piece to Mr. Forrest yourself," he went on. "But I could send it for you. Let him read it as it stands, since he knows the people mentioned. Then he can advise as to how it should be changed if he decides to use it."

"He'll send it right back," Melora said.

"All right—be a pessimist! But let me try anyway. And, Melora, you ought to attempt more of this sort of thing. I don't see any reason why you couldn't write for the magazines regularly if you really wanted to."

She stared at him in astonishment. In a few casual words he had opened a vista so astonishing, so enticing, that she was speechless.

"You've wanted something to do, haven't you?" he said. "You've been restless and not very happy and you've wanted something more to occupy yourself with than housework and sewing."

She nodded, pleased once more by his perception.

"You asked me a question yesterday," Tony said. "Do you remember?"

How could she forget? She had regretted her frank words more than once. Yesterday's spell, when she had sat in the rubble of that ruined house listening to his stories, was gone.

She jumped down from the wall, but Tony caught her by the arm.

"If you try to run away, I'll hold onto you. And think how that may look to anyone who happens to glance out a window. If you go struggling with me your mother may see fit to put me right out of the house."

He was laughing, but she turned back.

"Look at me," he said.

What she saw in his warm dark gaze sent a tingling to her fingertips.

"I'm not forgetting Quent," he told her. "Quent has been more of a friend to me in past years than I'd have expected, considering that we live on different hills. But I'm going to say this one thing. Then that will be all, Melora. I know you'll forget about me and marry Quent. And if I don't forget you for a while, that will be my own affair."

She could only wait for his words.

"History seems to have repeated itself," Tony went on lightly. "Just as a girl walked into my father's life one day in a bookshop, so a girl walked into mine. The circumstances were different. But as I came to know this girl a little better, I could see in her a great many qualities which I respected. Intelligence. Kindness. Courage."

He raised a hand and began ticking off her virtues, smiling with his lips, though he was serious.

"Integrity," he went on. "Melora, I believe you're the most completely honest person I've ever known. You deal in no tricks, no wiles. A fellow knows you're honest through and through."

Now she looked away. Because what he was saying wasn't true. Because of the hoax she had enacted with Quent she did not feel in the least an honest person. Yet how could she face him and tell him that her engagement to Quent was a lie? That she had deceived her own mother and Quent's father, Gran, himself, everyone? For no good reason. Just heedlessly, as a lark.

The important thing about being honest was to be that way even when honesty might injure oneself.

Yet she could not bring herself to speak. She could not spoil his words. No one else had ever spoken to her like this.

"Good night, Melora," he said softly as she moved away. She could not answer, but picked up her skirts and ran across the grass in the soft twilight.

No one seemed to have been looking out the windows. No one seemed to have known that she and Tony were in the garden together. The house was in a stir because of the miraculous Pacific cable which had been laid successfully only a few years before. A cablegram had just come through from Honolulu, brought to the house by messenger. Papa's ship would arrive the first week in June. And that was next week.

Mama was hugging the cablegram to her and laughing. Alec called from upstairs to know what the excitement was all about. Hardly noticed, Melora ran through the group and went upstairs to tell him. At the landing she turned and glanced down.

Over the heads of the others Quent was watching her, an odd expression quirking one corner of his mouth. Quent had seen her in the garden. But Quent, she thought as she hurried upstairs, did not matter.

15

BILLOWING SAILS

Even as a little girl Melora had never been able to give her affection as demonstratively as the rest of the family. Love for her father might be as strong as theirs, but she could not show it as easily.

Now it was like that again—an old scene re-enacted. They had promised Alec to bring Papa upstairs the moment he arrived and they were in Alec's room now. Papa sat at the head of the bed, with Alec leaning against him, and Mama and Cora both drawn into the curve of one arm. They were all talking at once. Mama was crying a little and laughing at the same time. It was even more moving than usual because of the trouble and worry behind them.

But as always Melora stood a little apart and waited. And as always her father's eyes met hers over the top of Cora's sunny head and told her without words that he loved her and that their own time together would come.

Of course there were gifts to be exclaimed over— a jade pin for Mama, a brocade belt with an ivory buckle for Cora's small waist, a carved puzzle for Alec, hatpins with ivory knobs for Gran, and a coral ring for Melora. Even Quong Sam received a handsome pair of ivory chopsticks from a special shop in Shanghai.

Papa sat there, tall and lean and quiet, the center of an excitement that bubbled around him. Melora thought how handsome he was in his blue uniform, with its touches of gold.

At length the talk and the laughter and confusion came to an end, and Melora said that there was something she wanted to show him. He came with her to her room, an arm about her shoulders, and she flung open the door, facing the shelf where Kwan Yin, her blue hair coiled smoothly atop her golden head, seemed to watch them in greeting.

Melora had never told him in a letter; she had waited, wanting the deep pleasure of this surprise.

His hand upon her shoulder tightened. Then he crossed the room, drawing Melora with him.

"I'd never thought to see her again. Thank you, my dear. Because of the friend who gave her to me, her value is very great."

Her head back against his tall shoulder, Melora nodded. "I know. I had to save her for you."

"There are so many things I want to hear," he went on. "I'll want every detail of what happened to each one of you during those days of the fire. But first I want to know about you, Melora. This engagement to Quent came as a surprise. Are you happy? Is this what you truly want?"

She had wondered how she would deal with this question when it came. Now she did not hesitate.

"I'm not really engaged to him," she said. "It started out as a silly game because we were tired of our mothers' matchmaking. I'm as much to blame as Quent because I went along with it. But I meant to clear it up right away when I came home from Chicago. Then the fire changed everything. Quent says to let things be while everything is so upset. But I wanted you to know the truth."

He seemed to understand as he always did. "I can see you have a problem on your hands. But I suppose I'm more relieved than anything else. A father usually thinks his daughter is too young for marriage. And Quent, much as I like him, has always seemed a bit irresponsible."

"He's changed a great deal," Melora said. "You'll hardly recognize him as the same boy."

"Does this make a difference in your feeling toward him?"

She hesitated, then shook her head. Lately, it was true, she had found herself taking Quent less for granted. But now she wanted to tell her father about Tony Ellis, and this she could not bring herself to do. Later, perhaps, after Papa came to know Tony. Not now, not so soon.

She told him instead about the long letter she had written him and now could not give him because Cora and Tony had sent it off to Mr. Forrest's magazine. Nothing had been heard of it since.

Her father did not seem to think the notion silly at all. "After all," he said, "I've been reading your letters for a long time. I know how good they are."

During the weeks that followed Captain Cranby was the center of all family activity. Everyone consulted him about every move. He and Gran had long sessions about matters of insurance, about the little trickle of boarding house income—since Quent and his father and Tony Ellis had remained as guests. And about other problems that were part of the new life of San Francisco. Even Uncle Will Seymour talked with him about the grave questions which faced him, but which looked now as though they might somehow be resolved, even though the Seymour fortune was gone.

As Papa pointed out, the name of the Seymour company still retained its reputation in the city. New buildings were going up, those which stood in skeleton form were being rebuilt and repaired, and no San Franciscan would be likely to allow new property to go long uninsured. With new insurance money coming in to companies like Will's, the prospect was not hopeless. Of course Uncle Will had thrown his own personal fortune into this and had been selling his paintings right along. Thus he would be able to pay off his debts in part. If people could be persuaded to wait for the rest . . .

Since there was no longer any hill of the nabobs in its former sense, Mama had become temporarily a homebody. Papa said jokingly that he didn't expect that to last, but all in all it was wonderful to have Papa home!

The day came, as Melora knew it would, when the two of them went off for an afternoon alone.

"Where shall we go?" he'd asked her and she'd answered readily.

"The Plaza, I think. If there's anything left. I haven't been back to see."

The custom of visiting Portsmouth Square had begun when she was a little girl. First there was always a trip to Chinatown, with its sights and smells, then downhill to the old Plaza, around which the first buildings of San Francisco had sprung up, Spanish fashion. Portsmouth Square, it had been named, after the United States sloop which had first run up the American flag at the little settlement of Yerba Buena on San Francisco Bay. It was there that Stevenson's *Hispaniola* sailed atop its monument.

They'd gone by cable car in the old days, but the cables were not yet running into that part of town, so since Quent had an errand to do for his father down on the Embarcadero, they drove with him in the buggy.

Papa observed the ruins with interest, but without sentimentality. Like Gran, it was always his philosophy to put the past behind him and walk cheerfully in the present. Chinatown was no more, and that was a great pity. But in the bright clear light of the June afternoon, its streets were alive with workers, clearing debris, dismantling. The noise of tearing down and putting up was everywhere. From any quarter at any time might come explosions as ruins were dynamited.

There was little of the old peace that had once graced Portsmouth Square. Tents were pitched throughout the square, hiding paths that rayed from the center. The Chinese and Italians particularly had found a haven here.

"Shall I wait while you look around a bit?" Quent asked. "Or shall I come by for you on my way home in an hour or so? Doesn't look as though there's much to do around here."

That seemed true at first glance. On every side ruin hemmed the square—the skeleton buildings, the piles of brick and rubble, the sickish stench that would haunt San Francisco for a long time to come.

"Shall we stay or go?" Melora's father asked.

"Let's stay," she said. These paths at least were old San Francisco. Besides, there was still something she must see.

So Quent went off without them and they threaded their way among tents and crowded benches, moving always toward the magnet of the square's center. The leaves on the trees had been scorched, but the shrubbery was still green, and everywhere leaves shimmered green and trembled in the breeze.

Melora walked on toward the arch of poplars where the rayed paths met. Beneath shielding

branches the little galleon sailed, golden pennant flying, sails billowing full in a wind that never died.
Stevenson's *Hispaniola* was immortal.

Melora sighed her relief. "It's as Tony said. The
ship sailed away the night the fire came. Danger
couldn't touch it."

"What would you like to do now?" her father
asked.

Melora's eyes lifted to nearby Telegraph Hill. On
its top she could see the wreckage of another fire.
Some years before a curious structure known as Lay-
man's German Castle had been erected there. But it
had never been very popular as a restaurant and a
few years ago it had burned down. Clinging to the
cliffs below were a handful of little houses which
had survived a far worse fire.

"Let's go up there," Melora said on sudden impulse. "Tony's grandfather has a restaurant that
wasn't burned down in the fire. Lombardi's. And
his mother's living there now. I'd like to say hello to
her."

Her father was willing, so they left the square and
started up the steep slope.

"Tell me more about Tony Ellis," her father said
as they followed the middle of the street.

She had wanted to talk to him about Tony ever
since he had come home. He'd had time to observe
Tony himself by now and she wanted very much to
know what he thought of him. She told him of that
day on Van Ness when Tony had auctioned off the
burned books. Of the time with Alec, and the story
of Tony's father and Lotta Lombardi.

Disappointingly, her father made no comment.
Whatever his own opinion of Tony might be, he did
not betray it, and she could not ask. Instead, he began
to talk about Quent and the new interest he was
taking in his father's business.

"Do you think," Melora broke in at last, "that people can really be changed by a happening like this? Sometimes Quent seems different. But other times he's just as he used to be and I don't see any change at all."

"Not changed, necessarily," her father said. "It seems to me that a terrible disaster may serve to test a man, to bring out qualities he already has, whether good or bad. I remember reading something while I was at sea, after news of the earthquake and fire had reached me. Something the old philosopher Seneca once wrote: 'Fire is the test of gold; adversity, of strong men.' I'm inclined to think that when strong men are tested, they show the gold."

"Like Gran," said Melora and did not return again to the subject of Tony or Quent.

The lower slopes of Telegraph Hill were as grim as the rest of the city, but as they mounted steeply a haven of green bowers hung above them. Houses clung precariously to the cliff amid vines and shrubbery. In small gardens hung cages with yellow canaries in them, and everywhere the riotous red and pink geraniums made a splash of color. After the desolation below, this spot seemed unbelievably brilliant and gay.

"It's not real," Melora said. "Someone has painted it there."

Papa smiled. "There's the Lombardi place just above us. I've dined there a few times long ago. Shall we go up?"

They started up a steep flight of steps. This visit would be something to tell Tony about.

"I expect Tony seems rather an exciting young man, to you and Cora," her father said as they climbed.

"He certainly seems exciting to Cora," she said carefully. This, at least, was no secret. Cora flirted

openly with Tony and it seemed to Melora sometimes that Tony was altogether too ready to play
the same game.

"I've noticed," Papa said. "But I wasn't thinking
altogether of Cora."

She went ahead without answering.

It was Mrs. Ellis who saw the visitors from her
vantage-point on a narrow veranda and called out in
delighted greeting. By the time they reached the veranda, an old man had come out to welcome them
and Melora gathered that this was Tony's grandfather.

Antonio Lombardi had black hair and a flourish-
ing black mustache, at which he tugged when he
was particularly enthusiastic. His was the warm
and fluent nature of the Italian homeland and he
shook Captain Cranby's hand heartily, then took
both Melora's hands in his and squeezed them till
she could feel her bones creak.

This was a great joy, an honor, he cried. His
daughter, his grandson, owed their very lives to Captain Cranby's family. The debt of the Lombardis was
enormous and he would accept no denial. But how
fortunate that they should come here this very day.

"Is most fortunate, no?" He prodded his daughter,
who nodded in agreement.

It seemed that Papa Lombardi was planning to
open his restaurant again—perhaps for two nights
a week. The roads were clear enough for cars and
carriages to make the trip. And where in all San
Francisco was a fine meal to be had these days? The
Poodle Dog was gone. Gone was Papa Coppa's. But
there were those who were tired now of earthquake
fare and who longed for such a meal as only Papa
Lombardi could prepare in his restaurant here on
Telegraph Hill.

"But firs'," he went on, "it is for my friends that

I give the beeg dinner. You be here nex' week, Cap'n Cranby? You come, I give the beeg party."

"Of course," Papa promised. "I'd be delighted to come."

Mrs. Ellis explained further. "My father means of course that you are all to come. Everyone in the Bonner house. Your grandmother, Miss Melora, your mother. Mr. Seymour and his son. Your sister. And of course, my Tony. You will tell him, please?"

Melora was puzzled. Why should she make a special point about Tony? Obviously her son would come.

"Of course I'll tell him," she said. "Of course we'll all come."

The old man was silent and Melora suspected a displeasure that she did not understand. Mrs. Ellis must have noted it.

"We will be very happy if my son comes," she said. "Please try to persuade him."

"Why should he need persuading?" Melora asked blankly.

Papa Lombardi snorted. "That Tony gets the swell-in-the-head. He think we smell too much of the fish and the spaghetti sauce. But his Uncle Vito fish—so sure he smells lika fish. And how you think you cook Spaghetti Lombardi and no put in what makes the so wonderful smell?"

"I—I'm sure I don't know," Melora said, a little taken aback. "And I'm quite sure Tony will come. I'll promise you that."

"My Tony did not like it when I came to live here with my papa," Mrs. Ellis explained. "He has not come here to visit me since I left your house."

"I'm sorry," Melora said. "I didn't know that." This was something she did not understand and which carried embarrassing undercurrents. She was relieved when Papa Lombardi said he must show them about the place. A place that was now practically a museum—a remnant of *old* San Francisco.

They had trouble tearing themselves away and returning to Portsmouth Square in time to meet Quent. But the interlude had been fun and by the time they got home Melora was eager to see Tony and tell him of their visit. She felt she could dismiss the odd things his grandfather and his mother had said as the words of an older generation likely to fuss over new ways.

16

ON TELEGRAPH HILL

Tony's dismay, his almost surly silence over the plans for the Lombardi party, came as a surprise to Melora in spite of Mrs. Ellis' words. At first he said flatly that he would not go. His attitude was almost one of being offended because such a party was to to be given. But he would not explain or offer a reason for the way he felt.

It was Cora in the end who coaxed him into going. Cora could charm the knob off a bedpost, as Gran sometimes said. They all needed a party, Cora pointed out. San Francisco was growing unutterably dull. After the excitement of the earthquake and fire, life seemed very tame when there was nothing to do but work and go around showing how brave you were all the time. She, for one, was very tired of being brave. She couldn't stay excited forever about donkey engines and pile drivers. She wanted some *fun*. And this party wouldn't be fun at all if only the older people went.

Tony smiled and Cora went right on.

"I've always loved Telegraph Hill. The view up

there is so wonderful. Perhaps we can get away during the evening and climb right to the top where we can see everything."

Tony's ill-humor vanished. "Telegraph Hill it shall be," he said. And Melora, who was watching, saw him look away from Cora's merry face and meet her eyes directly. It was an eloquent look that was almost a signal, a challenge. She was not at all certain what to make of it.

Papa Lombardi was making a big thing of this re-opening. It was a good opportunity for publicity. The newspapers would be glad to report a social function for a change, especially when such a function would be held right in the middle of San Francisco's ruins.

There was considerable to-do in the Cranby household over the matter of dress. Not that one looked askance at any manner of costume these days, but women folk liked to be beautiful and there were, after all, party dresses from Melora's trunk. None of these would fit Mama, but Mrs. Cranby was able to compromise by earing a frilly peekaboo shirtwaist of lace with her everyday skirt, and her new jade pin at her throat. There was a green frock that went well with Cora's blond prettiness, while Melora wore her favorite gown of lilac satin, with yards of flounces around the bottom and tiny bows of lilac velvet trimming on the bodice. Gran bought a new lace collar to go with her black dress and would wear the garnet earrings which Henry Bonner had given her.

There was something of a scene in the afternoon when Cora insisted on putting up her hair. She would not, she announced—she would absolutely not!—go to this party with her hair down her back in a schoolgirl curl and a hairbow. Mama said Cora was really only a baby and she couldn't bear to see her children growing up, but Papa came to Cora's aid and the matter was settled.

Melora worked over her sister's hair for an hour, with Mama and Gran helping, and even Quong Sam criticizing the fashionable pompadour as being too "floppy." At length, with tortoiseshell combs and hairpins, Cora's graduation to adult status was achieved and Melora had to admit that she looked very grown-up and strikingly pretty.

There was one small worry at the back of Melora's mind. Mama had heard from Nell Forrest and had reported that Nell and her son Howard were going to attend Papa Lombardi's dinner. Nothing had happened about the account Melora had written and Tony had mailed to Mr. Forrest at the magazine. Tonight she would have to meet the editor and perhaps discover exactly what he thought of her effort. Somehow she was more concerned because of Tony than because of her own feelings in the matter. She herself knew what the result was sure to be. But Tony had been so confident.

Alec was heart-broken because he was too young to go to the party, though he was up now and hobbling around on crutches. But Quong Sam could be counted on to keep him entertained for an evening.

It took both the Seymour car and the buggy to get them all to Telegraph Hill. By zigzagging, the buggy reached the foot of the steps leading to the restaurant. But the car coughed and died on a steep slope and everyone had to get out and walk.

Melora had been paired with Quent, while Cora had made it her business to annex Tony. He'd been especially flattering about the new hair-do and Melora suspected that Cora's hair was now up for good, no matter what Mama said.

The big main room of the restaurant reached

across the front of the building, overlooking the bay area. The Golden Gate was out of sight over the top of the hill, but the lights of Berkeley and Oakland twinkled across the bay, and Yerba Buena Island made a small patch of blackness on the water.

Lombardi tables wore red checked cloths and there were candles in big bottles half hidden beneath melting layers of colored wax. Fish nets looped across the ceiling to add atmosphere and on the walls were hundreds of drawings—caricatures of famous folk drawn by local artists.

But the most important, most colorful piece of all was Tony's grandfather. He was everywhere at once, joking and laughing, hearty and uninhibited. Tony's Uncle Vito was there tonight too, helping out as a second host, and where Uncle Vito was, Melora discovered, there was likely to be a strong smell of fish. She saw the wrinkling of Tony's nose, saw the way he edged back and stood in the shadow, as if he did not want to be connected with these relatives on Telegraph Hill.

Was he ashamed of them, she wondered, and tried at once to dismiss the idea. He couldn't possibly be scornful of this old man who warmed the entire place with his kindness and good will.

She was glad to see Quent talking boats with Uncle Vito. Mrs. Ellis' brother was obviously more at home with the business of catching fish, and this matter of greeting strangers made him uneasy.

The Forrests were already there and were to sit at the Cranby table. But the table was a long one and to her relief Melora found herself nowhere near the editor. She sat between Quent and Uncle Will Seymour, with Tony and Cora down at the other end. Mrs. Ellis had the place beside Papa and was already talking to him like an old friend. Tony's mother looked especially beautiful and dramatic tonight in wine red satin with rhinestones sparkling at her neck.

But it was the fresh crabs, the Spaghetti Lombardi, the ravioli and crusty Italian bread that held first place in everyone's attention for a while. Surely there had never been a gayer party given in all San Francisco. Both ladies and gentlemen wore everything imaginable—and no one minded. Stories of earthquake and fire were exchanged gayly and the talk was of the beautiful city that was to rise again here beside the bay.

When they had eaten as much as they could hold, someone started a call for Lotta Lombardi. Mrs. Ellis clasped her hands to her heart and shook her head vehemently. Her voice was long gone, she protested. She could not possibly sing—a thousand times no! But sing she did, in a voice that had not entirely lost its beauty. First an aria from *Madame Butterfly*, then an Italian folk song or two, and finally a snatch of popular music, with everyone joining in.

Afterwards there were impromptu speeches. Bouquets were tossed at Papa Lombardi, and Papa Lombardi tossed bouquets at his guests. There was much laughter and applause from the tables.

Among others, Howard Forrest was called upon to speak as editor of the California magazine, *Mission Bells*. Mr. Forrest told them that the rest of the world still did not believe what San Francisco could do.

"When oh-six goes out," he said, "we'll be well on our way to realizing a brand new city. This will be the biggest New Year celebration ever. Some of the big downtown buildings will be open again. And it won't be long before the Fairmont will be taking in guests. There'll even be a new Palace and the St. Francis will move out of its makeshift quarters in Union Square. All this while the rest of the world is pitying us and pulling long faces about the length of time it will take us to recover."

He went on to say that his magazine was doing its best to give the country a true picture of what had happened and what was happening here. Among the accounts he was running there was one outstanding piece which had been written by a young lady who was here tonight. Perhaps it wasn't fair to spring this on her without warning, but it was rather fun. Of all the pieces that were now reaching him, this was one of the most humanly written. Reading it you could almost smell the smoke and feel the rain of cinders, but you could hear a heart beating too— the heart of San Francisco. He wanted very much to present to them Miss Melora Cranby, author of the article.

Melora sat frozen at her place, turning hot and then cold, not knowing which way to look or what to do. From across the table Mama was waving at her to get up, to say something. She was aware fleetingly of Tony's triumphant smile and her father's pleasure, of Gran's look that was somehow not surprised, but very proud. It was Quent who came to her aid.

"Just get up and smile and say 'thank you,' " he whispered and helped to pull back her chair.

She could manage that much, though all the faces and smiles seemed to dance before her. Then she sat down while applause rang through the big room.

The formal part of the dinner ended after that. Mr. Forrest left his place and came directly to speak to Melora.

"You'll be receiving a letter from me in a day or two," he said. "With our check, of course. We're making a few changes if you agree—just to remove the personal touches in the piece. And, Melora, while this was one of those natural subjects you might handle rather easily, I feel that you have talent for this type of writing. I want to talk to you about these things soon, my dear."

He squeezed her hand and she could only murmur another thank-you before he went back to his place.

"Well, don't look so stunned," Quent said. "We've always known you were smart. Maybe we've another Gertrude Atherton in our midst."

His banter helped and her senses stopped whirling so that she could settle down a little and look at this wonderful thing that had happened to her. Not that it was to be believed yet—not wholly. And she couldn't even think of the possibilities it might open to her. The prospect was too dizzying. Thank goodness Papa was still here. She'd have a long talk with him tomorrow.

17

TONY

People were turning away from the long tables, moving about the room to talk and visit, while Papa Lombardi and his waiters brought them coffee.

Mama rushed over to hug Melora; Gran said they were proud of her but that this was just a beginning to some good hard work; and Papa said more with his deep, quiet look than anyone else managed with words. It was lovely to have them all so pleased and proud. She looked around for Tony and saw him talking to one of the guests who had known his father. He gave her a quick salute of approval.

Cora, as excited tonight as Mama, caught her sister about the waist and whirled her in circles until all the lavender bows on Melora's dress danced too.

"There—you see! Now aren't you glad I gave that letter to Tony?" Cora cried, and Melora had to admit breathlessly that she was.

Cora looked about the room and spoke in a conspiratorial whisper. "Maybe this is our chance to run away from the party and climb to the top of the hill. We can't be on Telegraph Hill and not go to the top. Let's see if the boys are willing."

Melora was happy enough where she was, but a

breath of fresh air would be nice. And she would like being nearer Tony than she'd been all evening.

When the boys agreed, they got into their wraps. The two girls tried veils over their heads, knowing it would be blowy on the hilltop. Tony, who knew every inch of the hill, led the way up a winding path.

Cora followed close on his heels while, as usual, Melora fell back with Quent, who was in no hurry and never one to gallop up a hillside. Trees arched over the path and the smell of green things was strong enough to mask the burned odor that was always on the wind.

It was a brilliantly clear night, with the fog horns silent and a full moon shining through the dark leafiness overhead.

"Melora!" Quent called and she paused in her effort to keep up with Cora's swift pace.

She turned and waited in a clear, moonlit space on the path. He came up to her, oddly solemn for Quent, and before she knew his intent he put a hand on each arm and bent to kiss her, lightly, quickly. This was a Quent she did not know.

"There," he said, still serious. "That's because I'm proud of you. And because I won't have another chance. You can give me back my ring now, Melora."

"But—I thought . . . I mean, you said—" she faltered.

"Of course if you want to make our engagement official"—he was smiling now—"I'll be a gentleman and oblige. But if you want to be let off—"

She took the ring from her finger and gave it to him. None of this made any sense. Why should he suddenly decide on this course, when he had seemed so set against it before?

"People will say I'm throwing you over because

of—of what has happened to your father," she reminded him.

Quent shrugged. "The ones who count will know better."

"Has Papa been talking to you?" Melora asked.

He shook his head. "No one has talked to me. I've just been using my eyes, that's all."

She didn't know what he meant, but Cora called to them from the top of the path and they went on. Eventually, Melora supposed, Quent would get around to telling her why he'd come to this decision. But for the moment she could only feel a sense of relief and release. Her hand was bare of the make-believe sign she had worn. It was bare for Tony to see.

Tony and Cora were waiting below the ruin of the "castle" which had once raised its bastions near the top of the hill.

"Shall we go on?" Tony asked.

Quent seated himself lazily on a low stone wall and pulled Cora down beside him before she could resist.

"No, thanks," he said. "I've had enough of looking at ruins. You two go ahead. Cora will keep me from pining away."

"I will not!" Cora cried and started to her feet. But Quent held her deliberately beside him.

"Yes you will, my poppet. Granpa wants to talk to you for a minute. There's a thing or two you need to know."

Cora stayed.

"Come along," said Tony to Melora.

They climbed to the crest. The wind struck them, whipping at Melora's skirts, tearing at her veil. There was a cool, bracing sting to its thrust that whipped cobwebs from the mind and filled the lungs with clean, sea-borne air.

"Cora is a most determined young lady," Tony

said, laughing a little, but before she could speak he went on to other matters. "It's wonderful that Mr. Forrest liked your piece. We're all proud of you."

"Thanks to you," Melora said. "I can't really believe in it yet—all the possibilities it opens up. I've been longing to do something. Perhaps this is it."

"There ought to be more of an escape for you than into words," Tony said.

She didn't know what he meant. He brushed her arm lightly with his fingers and all her senses were aware of his touch.

"Look," he said.

The hill slanted steeply from beneath their feet. The view in the moonlight was both beautiful and a little terrifying. There were isolated patches of light in the darkness, and there were rings of distant light cut off by the hills. But for the most part the streets ran like straight white lines beneath the moon, ruled beween strips of dead black. High across the dark valley a tiny cluster of lights shone on Russian Hill.

"They saved Mrs. Stevenson's house on Russian Hill," Tony said. "A little triangle of other houses escaped too. But the house my father built is gone. It was a small house just beyond those we can see."

"I'm sorry," Melora said.

"There was a whole room in it filled with books," Tony mused. "I used to lie on my stomach before the fire in that library for hours at a time when I was small, reading and dreaming about all I'd do when I grew up. About how I'd *be* somebody important and make everyone pay attention to me. Mama was sure I'd ruin my eyesight, but my father made her let me be. You know, I think she's almost glad the house burned down."

Melora glanced at him. "But why?"

"Well, she always lived the way he wanted to live while he was there. But afterwards it was only a shell of a house for her. She stayed because my father had wanted her to—because of me. But I'm sure she's happier here with my grandfather and the others. She loves the excitement and laughter and tempers and tears. But I—well, I'm more like my father."

Melora wondered how true that was and if he might not be fooling himself a little. Tony liked excitement too. She didn't want to see him turn against his own people.

"Your grandfather is a wonderful person," she said. "I'm sure his heart is as big as the bay, and—"

Tony broke in resentfully. "When I was in school they used to call me 'wop' and 'dago.' But I belong to my father's side, not my mother's. I want to stay as far away as possible from people who speak broken English and try to make America just like the old country. I won't carry a handicap like that around with me!"

His words shocked her. Eddie Quong came to mind and she could see him bowing respectfully in his uncle's direction. She could hear the words he had spoken that day. *My uncle is old China. It is a fine thing to be old China.* Eddie, with his American college education, had still been proud of his uncle and the heritage behind him. It seemed to Melora that he was right.

She reached out with her hands, as if to encompass all the ash-strewn space below their hill. "I don't think America can ever be just one kind of people," she protested. "Couldn't you feel all the lively, boiling mixture out there during the days of the fire? We were all so different, and yet we were all part of the same thing. We all liked each other and were ready to help each other."

"Earthquake love!" said Tony scornfully. "It won't last."

"I don't believe that. I don't think we'll ever go back entirely to what we were before."

But she knew she hadn't convinced him and she was sorry. She sighed without realizing it and he swung her suddenly toward him.

"I didn't come up here to talk about these things," he said. He raised her left hand in the moonlight. "So Quent told the truth. He said he'd get his ring back tonight and clear the air of his make-believe. Why didn't you tell me before, Melora?"

So that was what Quent had been up to.

"How could I tell you I was a fraud when you'd said you admired my honesty?" she asked unhappily. "The whole thing began as a joke, but we kept getting more tangled up in it and it became harder and harder to explain it to everybody. I'm glad I can now."

He drew her into his arms and she went unresisting. "How foolish you are, Melora. How could you believe I'd think you a fraud because of something so silly as this? I knew you were what I wanted from the moment when you walked into the shop that day, and I haven't wavered once since then."

"But you—you don't really know me," she faltered.

"Oh, yes I do. You stand for the things I want, Melora. Maybe Nob Hill's not important to you, but it is to me."

Melora stiffened in dismay. "But that's foolish. We're not Nob Hill. And we're poorer than ever now. Besides—that's the wrong reason—"

"I'm not talking about money!" Tony cried, laughing and shaking her a little. "I'll take care of that myself. But I'm not going to stay tied to a background of Telegraph Hill."

She was bewildered by his outburst. Whatever she had expected from him, it was not this. But he tilted her chin and when he kissed her she no longer tried to think, to understand. This was something she had wanted and dreamed about. She could not question this moment with Tony's arms around her and his cheek rough against her own.

"We'll be married," he said. "We'll be married just as soon as I get my first real part in the theater. You know that I'm going to be an actor, don't you? Not just an actor of bit parts—but a star some day at the very top."

He held her away from him, smiling at her confusion. He was going much too fast, but she felt breathlessly happy without bothering about words.

"You'll have to get used to the fact that I'm a dramatic fellow," he told her. "I'll never move at Quent's pace. Oh, I don't mean that we must go down now and announce this to your family. I've sense enough to know they'd all be set against it. But if we can't win them over in time, we'll have to elope. How would you like that, Melora?"

She gasped and he kissed her again.

"Don't look so startled. Everything will work out. I've some irons in the fire right now. It won't be long before theaters will be opening up in San Francisco again, and all I ask is one chance to convince an audience of what I can do."

She knew without the faintest doubt that he could convince an audience as he could convince her.

He gave her a last kiss and then took her hand. "We'd better go back before they send out a search party."

Hand in hand they went down toward the place where they had left Cora and Quent. For a little while there was only the moonlit world, the warm clasp of his fingers on hers, and this moment of complete happiness.

Cora was nowhere in sight. Quent still sat there staring up at the stars. He stood up and stretched, the old mockery back in his voice as he greeted them.

"About time you remembered me. As you can see, I've been deserted by my fair companion. Well, do you two have everything fixed up? Are you into a new engagement, Melora?"

The betraying warmth rushed into her cheeks as Tony answered.

"Not officially, my boy," he said jauntily. "But thanks for your cooperation, Quent. And we'll appreciate your silence on the matter for a while."

"Granted, old chap, granted!" said Quent, equally carefree.

They said very little on the way downhill. Melora drew on her gloves, not wanting Mama to note the absence of her ring tonight. There'd be time enough for that tomorrow.

"Am I really engaged this time?" she asked herself wonderingly. Somehow she didn't believe it. It was a little like a play and she'd become involved with the action on the wrong side of the footlights.

18

A CHANCE
FOR TONY

The others were waiting for them by the time they reached Lombardi's. Cora was being very gay and bright. She did not look at Tony, and when Melora went near her she turned away.

As they started home Melora rode in the buggy with Quent and Tony, while Cora stayed near her father and came home in the car with her elders. Fortunately, the car started while rolling downhill. On the drive home the boys talked lightly about old times in school. Melora felt bereft of words.

Now and then she stole a look at Tony, liking what she saw, feeling a little tingly as she remembered his kiss. How strange that she and Tony had found each other. That was another accident of the fire.

She avoided Quent, even when they reached home and he told her good night gravely. She had the uncomfortable feeling that he was criticizing her.

In her room, dressed in her nightgown and ready for bed, she still felt wide awake. If she got into bed right away she knew her thoughts would only chase

about on one another's heels. Among other things
to think about there was the problem of Cora.

How seriously were her sister's feelings involved?
It wasn't fair to dismiss Cora's notions about Tony
as a "crush," just because she was younger. Melora
could remember a boy in school whom she had liked
for most of one year, though he had not returned
her interest. Now she could hardly remember how
he looked or what it was that had seemed so remark-
able about him. Yet his indifference had hurt deeply
at the time. Cora could be suffering equally.

She slipped into her wrapper and went down the
hall to Cora's room. Her tap on the door was light,
so she wouldn't rouse the house. There was no answer—only a stillness beyond the door that was like
a held breath.

"Cora," she whispered, "it's Mellie. Let me come
in for a minute."

"Go away!" Cora said in a voice filled with tears.

Melora turned the knob softly and stepped into the
room. She stood for a moment studying shadowy
outlines. Then she crossed the room and sat down
on the edge of Cora's bed.

"Honey," she said, "don't be angry. Don't be hurt.
Whatever it was Quent told you, I'm sure he made
a mess of it."

Cora flopped over on her stomach and buried her
face in the pillow. "Go away and leave me alone! I
don't want to talk to you. How was I to know that
Tony—that you—" She gulped and let the words go
unfinished.

Melora stroked her arm.

"Nothing's really settled yet," she said. "Tony
wants to go on the stage. And I believe he will too.
I think he wants that more than anything else."

Cora seemed not to hear her. "I know I've behaved badly. I know I've flirted and tried my best

to attract his attention. But, Mellie, you don't know how hard it is—being your sister."

"What do you mean?" Melora asked.

"Oh, you were always the smart one. When you're in a room people know you're there, even when you don't say a word. But they never pay any attention to me unless I make them."

"What nonsense!" Melora cried. "You're the pretty one I've always envied. Everyone loves you and likes to have you around."

"Being pretty isn't enough. I suppose that's why I do crazy things sometimes. Like jumping up on that box and helping Tony sell those books. I wanted him to notice me and think I was wonderful. But it wasn't any use. Quent says—"

"Quent's always leaping to conclusions. All he's done tonight is embarrass us all and—"

Cora turned on her side. "But Tony—how does he feel? About you, I mean?"

This was dangerous ground. "I don't know whether Tony himself knows exactly how he feels," Melora ventured after a moment. "Perhaps a person who dramatizes a lot thinks he feels strongly about whatever seems to be important at the moment." Her own words frightened her a little, even as she spoke them. If this were really true about Tony . . .

Cora pushed a fist into her pillow. "How can you be so callous about how Tony feels? You don't *care* about Tony the way I do!"

What use was there in saying, "Maybe I do care —maybe I'm afraid of caring too much"? Cora would not understand a caring in which there were questions and doubts. She was like Mama in that.

She whispered "Good night" to her sister and went out of the room as softly as she had entered it. Cindy, the rag doll, sat against a pillow waiting for her, and Melora put her up on the shelf beside Kwan Yin. Neither was any help to her at the moment.

You did and you didn't, she thought. You loved and you doubted. You went toward and you drew away. You were in rapture over a kiss and uncertain a moment later. So how could you possibly give someone else an indication of your own true feelings?

Her left hand had a light sensation about it and she rubbed the third finger, momentarily surprised at the absence of the ring she had worn for the last few months. What would Quent do with it now? Who would be the girl he'd give it to some day? A girl who'd have "mystery and allure," he'd said that time on the ferry. Remembering the remark he'd made about Kwan Yin, she thought whimsically that it would be the girl with blue hair whom he'd always wanted to meet. But it was Tony, not Quent, who troubled her now. More than an hour went by before she fell asleep.

The next day there was "commotion" aplenty. Right at the breakfast table she made her announcement in a firm, brave tone. She and Quent were not engaged, never had been, really. Now the joke was over and the ring had been returned. No, she wasn't "throwing Quent over," and he wasn't "jilting" her. This was simply the dissolving of a very bad joke. She was sorry, but that's the way it was.

Mama turned pale and began to cry, and Cora had to run for her smelling salts. Uncle Will looked sorry. It was a good thing Papa jumped in and helped her out, for Quent lifted not a finger to come to her assistance and share the blame. In the end, however, it was Quong Sam who surprised her most.

He'd been serving breakfast while this was going on. When the meal was over and Papa had taken her mother upstairs for a talk, he pattered after Melora, his pigtail swinging.

"You no gotchee blains," he said. "You velly stupid ge'l." He waited for no response, but went off toward the kitchen, leaving her staring after him.

Gran and Cora had added nothing, either by way of protest or defense. Cora would hardly eat and she flushed miserably when Tony tried to tease her in his usual way. After breakfast she hid in her room and would see no one but Gran. Melora had an unsatisfactory talk with Mama and knew it was the first of many.

Late in the afternoon she found Gran sitting on the back porch steps shelling a pan of peas with Cora. They had been talking quietly and Cora looked up at her sister with the flicker of a smile. Never in her life had Cora been able to stay mad at anyone, though that didn't mean her hurt had lessened. Now she was ready to be friends again.

Down in the garden Alec and Matt, who often came over to play, were building a doghouse for Smokey and carrying on a loud-pitched argument on a subject commonly debated all over town. Melora listened in amusement.

"Market Street's done for," Matt announced authoritatively. "It's dead and buried. My Pa says. Fillmore'll be the big street, you'll see."

"That's not true," Alec cried with equal vigor, waving his hammer and chanting a popular jingle.

> Market Street was Market Street
>   When Fillmore was a pup;
> Market will be Market
>   When Fillmore's swallowed up!

Melora applauded, laughing, and her brother grinned at her.

"Sit down here," Gran said to Melora, tapping a step with her foot. "We're talking about love."

Melora went to sit on the steps below her.

"I was just saying," Gran went on, "that most folks make love a whole lot more complicated than it really is. There're only two ways about it, when you get right down to brass tacks. You either fall in love with a person for what he really is, or else you fall in love with your own notion of what he is. Those two things can be poles apart, but the trouble is they feel exactly the same in the beginning. It's just the endings that are so different."

Cora tilted her chin rebelliously. "I suppose you're thinking about Tony. I suppose you mean that I like Tony for things I only think he is."

"I didn't say a word about Tony," Gran said airily and popped a fat pod so that green pellets clattered into the pan in her lap. "I was just talking about love in general."

Melora picked up an empty pod and sniffed its moist green scent. "Maybe it's not really as clear-cut as all that, Gran. I mean no one we love is going to be absolutely perfect, any more than we ourselves are. For instance, there are a lot of things I could admire about Tony. But I could never admire the way he feels superior toward his grandfather and his Uncle Vito."

"Maybe not, but you could understand it, and forgive it," Cora said. "He told me about the way the kids in school used to tease him and call him names. Maybe we'd feel the same way in his shoes."

Gran nodded. "Probably would. I can remember a pile of things I felt tragic about when I was young. I had a feeling I'd been singled out especially by a cruel destiny. That was before I found out that most everybody else thinks he's been singled out too. When

I caught onto the fact that I was in such good company, I stopped feeling sorry for myself."

"Anyway, it doesn't make me like Tony any the less," Cora retorted stanchly.

"You'll recover," said Gran. "That's the one sure thing about a broken heart, in case that's what you're harboring. And don't dream over those peas or Sam is going to come out and fire the three of us."

Melora laughed and the moment of seriousness passed.

That week was a busy one, for Papa's ship was sailing on Saturday and there were endless things to do and say.

Melora was grateful for the talk he managed with her about her writing.

They were sitting in her room.

"It's a common experience for young people to feel an urge to escape from the familiar aspects of their lives," he said. "But, Melora, escape may sometimes be right there in your own heart and mind, and not depend at all on a mere change of scenery, or new companions. This writing talent may be the answer for you."

Of course if she meant to buckle down and take it seriously, he pointed out, it would mean hard work and a lot to learn. Hours of just writing every day, probably.

"You can put some of it into letters to me," he said, smiling. "Not only writing about things that happen, but about how you feel and think. I expect Howard Forrest will tell you that's the most important, and perhaps the hardest part."

There was a little silence and she plunged then into the subject she knew she must discuss with him before he went away. The fact that Tony had suggested marriage at some time in the future.

He listened gravely and when she was through he

asked a single question. "Are you sure this is what you want, Melora?"

She couldn't give him a clear-cut answer. "That's the trouble—one minute I'm ready to say 'yes,' and the next minute I don't seem to be sure."

He looked relieved. "Don't worry about it then, my dear. But don't do anything till you are sure. Sooner or later you will be, you know."

There had been times when she had felt that her father was not exactly enthusiastic about Tony. She had half expected protest from him.

"You mean you wouldn't oppose my marrying Tony?" she asked directly.

His smile was rueful. "I'm almost inclined to think the Chinese way is the best—when someone who is old and wise weighs all the aspects and brings together two young people so eminently suited to each other that they are sure to fall in love after they are married."

Melora must have looked shocked, for her father laughed.

"I know—this is America. I wish it were possible for a parent to go right on saving his children from hurt just as he did when they were little. But you're old enough now to take the responsibility for your own actions. Of course your mother may not feel that way."

Melora was quite sure of that. Mama had gone right on wailing over the "broken engagement" as it was. She would probably collapse completely if she were asked to accept Tony in Quent's place.

"Could we just not tell her for a little while?" Melora asked.

"It may not be necessary to tell her at all," Papa said thoughtfully.

So it was left at that. Though he had argued neither for nor against, Melora knew that her father hoped she would not marry Tony. And this made a deep impression.

After Papa's ship sailed, the house settled to routine again, and the summer days ran along pleasantly, busy and full, with Melora spending a couple of hours every morning alone in her room writing. Mostly it was just a sort of talking to herself in her diary. She wrote in it copiously every day now. These were the times she looked forward to more than anything else in her day. The diary writing gave her practice and it was an idea storehouse besides.

Her meetings with Tony were a mixed blessing. He affected her in a way that was often disturbing. There were moments when, if he had said, "Let's not wait—let's run off and get married now," she would have gone with him. She was happiest, however, when he asked nothing, but did thoughtful little things which revealed an understanding no one else had ever shown her. These were the times when she was most convinced of their affection for each other. Though she sometimes wondered if he were not playing the role of the perfect suitor without recognizing it himself.

As for Quent—he was working so hard in his father's business, often late into the evenings, that she saw him mainly at meals. He never teased as he used to do; he just kept out of her way. She couldn't help feeling a little hurt. They'd been friends for a long time and there seemed no reason for this new attitude.

There was excitement on the day *Mission Bells* appeared with Melora's piece, illustrated with several photographs of the fire. It seemed to read so much better in print. Everyone in the house had a turn at the copy, and the neighborhood was scoured for others. At Mama's insistence a copy was kept on the parlor table, so it would be there for any visitor who came in to see. But Melora had begun to have the feeling that its publication didn't mean much unless she could repeat the success.

In September Alec went reluctantly back to school and one more phase of everyday existence was reinstated.

Then one night something happened. Tony came home with news that was plainly elating to him. He said nothing at dinner, though Melora was aware of his inner excitement. Afterwards they sat on the low wall in the garden and he made his announcement dramatically.

"I've got it, Melora—a place in a theatrical stock company! I've tried out and they're taking me. I'm on the stage!"

She hadn't realized that he was doing anything so definite about an acting job.

"Tell me about it," she said.

"Well, for a starter, it's much better than being in one play. A play could be a failure and I'd be stranded wherever it opened. But this way I'll be working every week for months—in fact, as long as they like me, or as long as I want to stay."

"Then—you'll be leaving San Francisco?"

He looked at her contritely. "It has to be that way. But I'll be back before long. There are theaters opening again in this town and they tell me they'll probably book us into a stock theater some time this winter. Not too many companies will be playing San Francisco just now, so we should be welcome. But we're going to play a city or two in southern California first."

"What sort of parts will you have?"

"What they call the juvenile lead," he said. "That means I'll be the young fellow who always falls for the pretty girl who is the ingenue. Nothing very weighty most of the time. But I'll be getting experience. It's the first step, Melora. Will you miss me?"

Of course she would miss him, she admitted, already sensing the empty place his going would leave in her life. Where Tony was, there was always interest and excitement. Uncertainty too, perhaps, but never monotony.

There would be only a few months of this, he assured her comfortingly. Just enough time so he could be sure of himself and save up a little money. Then they could be married. He was going to hate this time away from her, but it couldn't be helped—it meant his future—their future. Of course when they were married she would come with him. He would be so proud to show her off as his wife.

She could feel a prickle of excitement as he pictured the adventurous life of an actor. Always new towns to visit, new parts of the country to see. And the adulation and admiration that was an actor's due when he was popular. Of course Tony Ellis was going to be popular. He would see to that. She had always wanted to escape, hadn't she? Well, this was the way.

His letters were hurried, but enthusiastic. They breathed his delight in the life of the theater. They spoke of her too and how much she meant to him. But even as she read his words the doubts came again. He wrote as he talked—dramatically, as if he could never stop imagining himself in a leading role. What if the time should come when he chose to play some other part?

He sent her one of his stage photographs, signed to her with love in a bold flourish. His smile flashed in the picture as it did in life and she longed with all her heart to be with him again.

Once he wrote that she might be able to get a place as a player of bit parts with his company. Such as the maid who dusted furniture in the first scene and gave the audience the lowdown on the family by talking things over with the butler. She might even use the name "Melora Bonner," and let it be known that she was the granddaughter of San Francisco's Henry Bonner. Of course it would be better for his own relationship with his audiences if they thought him unmarried. He had been advised of that by the girl who played the ingenue lead in his company. Mae Wentworth was not only a clever little actress, but she knew her way around theatrically speaking and had been of great help to him.

Melora dropped the letter to pose before her mirror with an imaginary feather duster in her hand, improvising gossipy remarks to a wardrobe closet. Melora Bonner, the onstage chambermaid! Then she caught Kwan Yin's smile and Cindy's faded look of wide-eyed surprise, and flung herself laughing on her bed.

"You're right," she told the two. "The last thing in the world I could ever do is sashay around a stage speaking silly lines to a butler." Write the plays, maybe, but not act in them. And as for borrowing prestige with her grandfather's name—no! It was her own name she wanted to give meaning to, but not over the footlights.

She tried to explain all this in her next letter to Tony, but by the time he answered he was off on another tack and didn't even mention the matter. She felt both exasperated and absurdly relieved.

The October rains were upon them now and sometimes it drizzled for days on end. Everyone else's spirits had a tendency to droop a little, but not Melora's. She had become deeply absorbed in a more ambitious piece of writing than she had dared to try before. This was something she might even show to Mr. Forrest.

19

MOMENTUM

It had begun as something in her diary—a little piece about Quong Sam and his nephew Eddie. But this time it wasn't just so many inanimate words on paper, as some of her efforts had been. This was alive and exciting. There was a pulse beat to it. She polished it up as best she could and sent it off to Howard Forrest.

Back it came, but with a letter of praise and encouragement. She was right—she had something here. But he'd like to see her enlarge it into an article that would cover more than the story of one Chinese servant in her own family. Let this be a piece about the experiences of other such families in San Francisco as well.

"Go to work and dig out more material," he wrote. "And send it back as soon as possible."

The letter came in the morning mail and knowing that it was her manuscript being returned, she had taken it to her room to open in unhappy privacy. But now she couldn't wait to share the news. Of course she would go to work on it—this very day, if she could.

She ran downstairs with the letter in her hand. Quent happened to come out of the drawing-room-office at that moment, and she waved the letter at him triumphantly.

"I've done it again! Or at least almost. Quent, look at this!"

For once he didn't bite her head off. He read the letter through gravely and gave it back to her. "How are you going to start? Getting your material, I mean?"

"I don't know. Oh, for the library! It breaks my heart when I think of all those books burning up. I thought I might talk to Sam a bit and try to—"

"Good idea. But I've got another suggestion for now. Come along with me on an errand I'm doing for Father. An old lady who has insurance with us is an invalid and I'm going out to talk to her. She's had Chinese servants all her life, and she'd probably love telling you stories about them. Hurry and get ready and we'll take a cable car. It's not far."

They had to run for the cable car, since you could never tell exactly where one would stop. Quent swung her up to an outside seat and she clung to the metal pole.

Down the steep hill they went, with Melora laughing as she slid on the slippery seat and was pushed back by Quent.

"Out for the curve!" shouted the conductor, meaning "look out," and with a great crashing and rattling and clanging of bells, they were off. They had the front of the car to themselves and Quent began to chant in Melora's ear. She joined in the words they'd both learned when Gelett Burgess had written *The Ballad of the Hyde Street Grip* a few years ago.

Oh, the lights are in the Mission, and the ships
  are on the Bay,
And Tamalpais is looming from the Gate, across
  the way;

The Presidio trees are waving, and the hills are
 growing brown,
And the driving fog is harried from the ocean to
 the town!
How the pulleys slap and rattle! How the cables
 hum and skip!
Oh, they sing a gallant chorus to the Hyde Street
 Grip!

They hopped off at their stop, still laughing, and
Melora realized that it had been a long time since
she'd laughed with Quent. She had missed the relationship she used to take for granted.

The elderly lady they were to visit received them
kindly in her wheelchair. Quent finished his part of
the business he had to transact and then Melora told
her hostess about her own problem. She could hardly have found anyone more willing to tell stories
about San Francisco's Chinese and her pencil was
busy jotting down notes. When they left she had the
names of other families from whom she could gather
stories.

"I'll love doing this piece," she told Quent as they
left the house. "There's been some feeling against
the Chinese and I'd like to make Mr. Forrest's read-
ers realize how wonderful they are. That's one of
the exciting things about writing—that you can actually influence people with what you write."

"I do believe you're turning crusader," Quent said.
But for once he wasn't laughing and she didn't mind.

Now, as they waited for the homeward-bound car,
Quent relaxed and talked about his father's insurance
business.

"To think I used to think it was dull and stodgy!"
he said. "I'm finding out that it's not just figures on
a sheet of paper—it's human beings, and all their

mixed-up problems. You know something, Melora —I've recently found out that I like people."

"I'd never have guessed it," she said, "by the way you've been snapping at me for the last few weeks."

"That's a woman for you. Always switching to the personal. I said 'people.' That doesn't include you. You're just one girl."

"Meaning you like people, but you don't like this one girl?"

He answered her almost roughly. "Maybe I like her too much. Maybe that's what makes me mad every time I look at her."

"But why should you be mad when you look at me? I don't understand."

"Tony," he said shortly. "Isn't that reason enough?"

This was more puzzling than ever. "But it was you who told him about our engagement not being real. It was you who—"

"I tried to hold out. I did my best that day in the park when I got you to keep on wearing my ring. But in the end I had to see the way things were. I had to do what you wanted me to—which was to get out of the picture."

Their car was coming, but he turned his back on it.

"Let it go. We can't talk if we get aboard. Now that we're launched on this subject I think I might as well finish. When I'm through you probably won't want to speak to me again, but I'm going to have my say."

The car clattered on its way. The street was empty and quiet except for the hum of the cables.

"What I want to say concerns Tony," he went on. "And I know how it will make me look. But I don't care, just so long as you listen to reason."

"Well, don't start shouting," Melora said. "I'm right here and I won't run away."

He flushed and lowered his voice. "I've known Tony for a long time and I know just what you mean to him. You mean Nob Hill and all it stands for. Things that are important to Tony. You mean someone to give him the self-confidence he lacks unless there is an audience—applause. Applause from you means a lot to him because of your background. This isn't something he thinks about. It's probably true without his knowing it."

Indignation began to rise in her. "You don't understand him at all if you can talk like that! For one thing, he's the most self-confident person I've ever met."

"So long as there's someone around to admire him and build him up, he is. But have you ever tried criticizing him?"

"There's never been any reason to. And I don't think you're fair—"

"I don't care whether I am or not. Look, Melora, Tony would be fine if he could just learn to believe in himself, to like himself. But it will always take someone else to give him this one thing he needs most. And I doubt that one person could do it forever."

"Well!" said Melora, really angry now and ready to defend Tony to her last breath. Having doubts herself was one thing, but when Quent attacked she could not endure it.

He went on however before she could speak. "I told you what you'd think of me. But I had to have my say. Now maybe I can stop being a grouch every time I look at you because I know somebody ought to tell you the truth and keep you from doing something foolish."

"I can't say I thank you," Melora said sharply. "And besides—I'm *not* Nob Hill."

"No, but you stand for what Tony thinks it stands

for. Just as I did when he first knew me. Never mind, save your words. I'll put you on the next car and let you go. I'm sure you don't want my company just now and I've thought of another errand I can do in this neighborhood."

She was glad enough to get on the car alone. It had begun to drizzle again and she went inside to keep dry. The ride home was no fun at all. Quent had spoiled everything. All she wanted was to get home to the seclusion of her own room where she could be good and mad in private.

Once there, she paced up and down mumbling angrily. Quent's outburst was completely unjust. He didn't really know what Tony was like, and she couldn't imagine what had got into him. The queer part of it was that in spite of how angry she was, there was a twinge of hurt because Quent had looked at her with such distaste as if he thought her merely foolish.

In the days that followed she and Quent were polite to each other, but that was all. She was glad to have her writing to throw herself into. She had found abundant material for her piece and there were more people to see than she needed. She rewrote the article three times before she dared send it to Mr. Forrest. Again it was returned, but only for revision. He was pleased with her industry and the way she had followed his suggestions, developing the idea even further on her own initiative. Editors, he said, liked writers who could pick up an assignment and carry it out satisfactorily.

A check came after the fourth revision and her success seemed more of a triumph than it had the first time, since she had really worked to prove her ability. The nicest part about it was that now she would have spending money for Christmas.

Her father was trying to save toward the building

of a new house that would be smaller than this one and would suit them better. The insurance money alone wouldn't be enough. They had lost too much. It looked now as though Mr. Seymour might rent the Bonner place from Gran and bring his wife and daughter home as soon as they could occupy it. So Papa wanted to get the building launched when he came home at Christmas time. Consequently they were not planning an elaborate Christmas.

Nevertheless, the holidays promised to be exciting. Mama was talking about giving a modest supper party on New Year's Eve. She felt they ought to be a part of the celebrations that would be held everywhere to greet 1907. "Oh-six" had had its terrors and triumphs, but now there was a sort of momentum which everyone in San Francisco could feel. A building up all through November and December because of the record rebirth of a city which would be climaxed on the eve of the new year.

Adding to the excitement for Melora was a lively letter from Tony. The thing he had hoped for was really going to happen. His company was to open in a rebuilt theater on Market Street during the week between Christmas and New Year's. Too bad he couldn't be home for Christmas, but of course he and Melora would celebrate New Year's Eve together.

It was even possible, he wrote, that the new year would bring an unexpected possibility for earning his way. Not a very important one, but something he might fit into his spare time. Nickelodeons were springing up all over the country and there were actors needed for the pictures which made up this new form of entertainment. So far most of these were produced in New York and Chicago, but Mae Wentworth, the actress whom he had mentioned before, said she'd heard of a company that wanted to start up right here in California. She herself hoped to play in one of their productions and she thought she might get him a chance too.

Melora was a little concerned over this plan. The nickelodeon was a cheap, not very dignified form of entertainment. Those flickering pictures would probably never become really important. But of course it was to Tony's credit that he wanted to try in every possible way to earn and to promote his own future.

She read the impersonal parts of the letter aloud to Cora, who always wanted—a little wistfully—to hear about Tony. Cora's reaction surprised her. Her sister pounced at once on the name "Mae Wentworth."

"Who's she?" Cora demanded. "Has he ever mentioned her before?"

"Of course he has," Melora said. "He has told me something about everyone in the company. I do believe you're more jealous than I am."

"I'm sure I am," said Cora tartly. "If I were you I'd keep an eye on his clever little actress."

Melora sighed as she put the letter away. She'd hoped that by this time Cora would have recovered from her notions about Tony. As old friends got in touch with one another once more, young people came and went in the house, and Cora was invited to a number of parties. But she went right on feeling that all the boys she knew were too young and foolish, and that there would never be anybody like Tony. Not that she was suffering acutely. Her naturally sunny nature had come to the fore and she was as gay as ever. But there were little moments when she betrayed herself. And she was outwardly more excited than Melora over the fact that Tony's company was to play in San Francisco.

In one way Melora could hardly wait to be with

Tony again. And yet she could not feel that she was truly ready for marriage. Her father had said that sooner or later she would be sure. But nothing had happened to clarify her emotions. She was, as far as she could tell, right where she had always been in her feeling about Tony. And was that good enough for the serious step of marriage? She knew her father would say it wasn't.

As Christmas drew near, however, she began to feel that this time would be the test. When she saw Tony, when she talked to him again, she would know. It had to be that way. She began to move toward their reunion with more confidence.

Quent's manner toward her had softened a little and he was making his own plans for the holidays. He had agreed to squire the two girls to the opening performance of Tony's company, mainly because Cora badgered him into it. He couldn't, he pointed out, though not ill-naturedly, be quite as thrilled about seeing Tony on the stage as they were. After all, he had been watching Tony perform on his own private stage for quite a few years. But there was another matter that Quent was looking forward to.

It had long been a San Francisco custom to promenade in carnival manner on New Year's Eve. Market Street had always been the scene of much gayety, with the loudest celebration centering at Market and Kearny. But this year Market, for all the rebuilding that was going on, would stand bleak and dark, while the New Year took over Fillmore and Van Ness. This would be the biggest celebration ever, if the prophets were to be believed, and he certainly didn't mean to miss it. So why not, he asked at dinner one night, all dress up in costume and go out to see the sights?

Mama said she disliked vulgar crowds and would stay home to oversee preparations for her supper party. But she supposed there was no reason why the young people couldn't have their fun. Melora wrote Tony to suggest that he come as he was in the costume of his play and join them after his New Year's Eve performance. Since Tony had gone on the stage, Mama was more prejudiced against him than ever and Melora tried to make this plan to see Tony seem casual. There was enough time to stir things up when they'd actually set a date for their marriage.

Papa's arrival—his ship was a couple of days early—solved the problem of costumes for the girls. When they opened their presents Christmas morning they found that he had brought them each a handsome Chinese robe of brocaded silk. Melora's was a golden yellow, with birds and flowers embroidered in sapphire blue, while Cora's was a delicate pale green, with a golden dragon curling down its back.

Papa had another surprise to announce on Christmas Day. He had been corresponding with Carlotta Ellis and had been to see her since he got home. She had agreed to sell him her plot of land on Russian Hill. Now that her son had gone on the stage, and she would never rebuild there, she would be happy to see the Cranbys take it over. So if they liked that, they could now build a house with a real view, instead of being tucked away low in the shadow of Nob Hill.

New Year's Eve fell on a Tuesday this year, and Tony's company was playing its first San Francisco performance the Saturday night before. Tony had written that they expected to be in early in the day and that he would come out to see Melora before rehearsal. But matters went wrong with the schedule and there was a delay about the arrival. He had only time to telephone her briefly before the late rehearsal was called.

The old tingle went through her when she heard his voice, so alive and familiar on the wire. But she was a little shy with him and hampered by the impersonal black mouthpiece. He was excited about the opening and pleased that she would see him for the first time in something that gave him a real opportunity.

"You're all to come backstage right after the performance," he told her. "I can hardly wait to see you."

Just hearing his voice made a difference. During the hours that intervened before they left for the theater, an increasing sense of sureness grew in her. She caught her father's troubled gaze upon her once or twice, but she could return his look confidently. Tonight she would really know.

20

BACKSTAGE

When the three walked down the main floor aisle toward their seats, Melora's anticipation increased until she was tense and a little nervous. Cora fairly sparkled with excitement, and only Quent remained unmoved. Since there was some uncertainty about what might happen tonight Melora couldn't help feeling more comfortable because Quent was there to see them through. Even though he didn't approve of Tony, he seemed to understand how she felt about him. She would miss Quent when she married and went away.

Their seats were good ones in the sixth row and Quent sat between the two girls. The house programs were rustling and Melora glanced at hers without seeing any name but Tony's.

Cora leaned toward her, tapping her own program. "There's that Mae Wentworth Tony wrote you about. She's playing the chauffeur's daugher."

Melora nodded, wishing the lump of tenseness inside her would dissolve. Why couldn't she relax and be casual about this whole thing? But then—how could she be casual when the outcome might mean that in a few weeks' time she would marry Tony and leave San Francisco for a new life? Now that the door was open she was almost afraid to step through it.

The house lights began to dim and as the theater darkened, the curtain went up with a whispering hush-hush, silencing the audience. Melora straightened in her seat. Cora leaned slightly forward, as eager as her sister.

Tony wasn't on in the first scene. There was the maid, busily swishing away with her fluffy feather duster, and Melora felt dreadfully like giggling. She could just imagine herself up there. Melora Bonner indeed!

A uniformed chauffeur was talking to the maid of the wealthy family for whom they worked, and in particular of the playboy son. That would be Tony, of course. The chauffeur announced menacingly that the young scion of the family had better keep away from his daughter or he would know the reason why. Then the principals, the stars of the company, came onstage as husband and wife, the parents of Tony. A round of applause greeted them.

As the play unfolded, Melora began to feel that it was rather silly and not very real. These people talked in an exaggerated manner and struck such ridiculous attitudes. Once she stole a look at Quent to see how he was reacting, but his expression gave nothing away. Beyond him Cora seemed absorbed.

The second scene showed an unbelievable backdrop of a garden scene, with the flower beds painted too brilliantly and the sky a flat blue with stationary clouds. Now Mae Wentworth came gracefully through the garden gate. There was no doubt that she was lovely, delicate, adorable, and quite at home before the footlights. The lines she spoke might be silly, but the audience loved her instantly.

In her role she was plainly looking for someone, as if she had a secret tryst, and when Tony came onstage she ran eagerly to meet him. Melora's hands tightened on the arms of her seat, her palms damp. This was the moment—now. That handsome, flashing young man up there on the stage was Tony. She waited for the electric moment of recognition, of conviction. But nothing happened. Mae Wentworth flung herself into his arms and Tony kissed her fervently to show how madly in love he was. He was behaving somewhat as he had that day when Melora had seen him on top of a packing box making the crowd on Van Ness do his bidding, winning them with his charm, leaping down to play the hero and rescue Alec.

On the stage all this seemed more convincing. Tony was good in his part. Around him there was somehow an aura of drama which made you believe what he wanted you to believe, whether you liked it or not.

It was plain that the feminine part of the audience adored him. He got a good hand of applause when he went off and Melora too applauded dutifully. Cora folded her own hands tightly in her lap and did not clap. Quent snorted impolitely.

When the first act was over Cora leaned across Quent to speak to her sister. "He needn't have kissed her so hard! I don't like that Mae Wentworth at all."

Melora laughed. "It's only a play, Cora. The actors don't mean what they're doing. And she's really very appealing. What did you think of Tony?"

"Oh, Tony's wonderful of course," Cora admitted readily. "It's just that I don't like the way he kissed that Wentworth person."

"Though nobody has asked me," said Quent, "I think this play is as hammy as any I've ever seen."

As the play went on, Melora began to feel uneasy. Tony was good, but he was doing something which made her uncomfortable. He was giving an exaggerated impersonation of what the son of wealthy parents might be like. Such a performance was puzzling. Why couldn't Tony have patterned his interpretation on what he knew from life? Money and position, or the lack of them, weren't all-important. Not all poor people were noble, nor rich people ignoble. Yet that, under and through the lines he spoke, seemed to be what Tony was implying.

The thing that troubled her most, however, was the fact that at no time while she watched him came a recognition of Tony as the person she loved. When the final curtain came down she wondered if she had been foolish to harbor such an expectation. It wasn't in some make-believe role that she could love Tony. It was for himself offstage. That or nothing. So perhaps the moment of recognition was simply postponed for a little while until they went back to his dressing room.

On the way up the aisle someone called to Cora and came toward them through a line of seats. It was a boy her sister had gone to school with—Harry Norman. They had not seen him since before the fire, and he had changed so much that she was surprised. He was taller and heavier, but more than that he had taken on a look of maturity.

Cora dimpled and summoned her gayest smile as she went ahead up the aisle with Harry.

"Well?" Quent said. "How do you feel now?"

"Feel?" said Melora. "How should I feel?" He saw too much; saw things she didn't want him to read —her continued confusion and uncertainty and doubt.

"One of these days," he went on as they stepped into the lobby, "you'll have to tell me what that last act was all about."

Melora did not answer and when Cora had told Harry goodby they went into the cool evening and around toward the stage door. The doorman let them through, waving them toward dim corridors and cubbyholes backstage. A smell of recently cut wood and fresh paint hung over the rebuilt theater.

Tony, seated before a mirror in a tiny dressing room, was removing his make-up. He wore a dark red robe, with a towel flung about his shoulders. When he saw them in the glass he jumped up to invite them in. He gave each girl a quick kiss on the cheek and held out a hand to Quent.

"How did you like it?" he asked confidently, as if only one answer were possible.

Cora didn't fail him. "You were wonderful, Tony," she said loyally.

He turned to the others questioningly, particularly to Melora.

Quent said, "Sorry, old fellow, but this isn't my type of show. I only came because I was bullied into it. I like dancing girls and more jokes."

Quent was clowning again, but Tony didn't care what Quent thought. He was still waiting for Melora's answer. She couldn't lie, however much he might want her praise.

"I—I'm afraid I didn't care too much for the play," she faltered. "But the company is very good. And you were good too, Tony. Though I couldn't agree with your portrayal of the part."

He looked both hurt and reproachful and she wished guiltily that she could have given him the unqualified praise he so plainly wanted. But before she could say more there was a "May I come in?" from the doorway and Mae Wentworth swept prettily into the room, still in costume. Her arms were full of yellow roses and she ran directly to Tony and kissed him.

"Thank you for the flowers!" she cried. "They're

lovely. Tony, your performance was fine tonight. I was so proud of you."

She seemed to note the others in the room for the first time. She still wore her stage make-up and at close hand it was too bright.

"I know," she prattled on, "—you're the friends Tony has told me about. The ones he stayed with during the fire. How nice that you could be here tonight. Wasn't he splendid?"

It was fortunate that Cora filled in with generous agreement what might have been an uncomfortable gap. Mae swept gayly out of the room, leaving a trail of perfume that dimmed the scent of roses.

"Quite a girl," Tony said. "And she's taught me a great deal about acting. She'll go places, that one."

"I've no doubt," said Quent dryly. He'd taken Cora by the arm and was moving her firmly toward the door. "We'll wait on the sidewalk outside, Melora. I need some fresh air. See you later, Tony."

Cora made no objection to being pulled away, though Melora almost regretted seeing them go. Nothing had turned out as she had expected tonight, and she could only feel self-conscious over being left alone with Tony. He seemed uncomfortable too and she realized that he was no more anxious to be alone with her than she was with him.

"You—you've changed, Melora," he said doubtfully.

Was that because she could no longer flutter in admiration of him? she wondered. Was it because, for the first time, she had openly criticized him? But one didn't change as suddenly as that, or for so small a reason. This was something that had been taking place in both of them during these months apart. Perhaps it was even something that had been deep in them all the time, hidden by surface emotions.

"Perhaps we've both changed," she told him.

"Perhaps we don't know each other very well after all."

He did not contradict that. From the make-up shelf before the mirror he picked up an eyebrow pencil and tossed it in his hand. He seemed to have nothing more to say, almost to be waiting for her to go.

It was possible, she thought a little sadly, that he could be quite ruthless if he chose. All the thoughtful little things he had done for her—that rose in the garden, his quick gift of the charred *Treasure Island* —had these been to please his own notion of himself in the role of a sensitive lover, as much as they had been to please her?

"You'll be with us on New Year's Eve, won't you?" she asked. That invitation had been made. It still lay between them.

He dropped the eyebrow pencil among the litter and turned back to her. "About that, Melora—I hope you'll let me off. Something terribly important has come up. Miss Wentworth has managed to get me an invitation to a pretty exclusive party given by the people who are going to make those nickelodeon pictures I told you about. This is an opportunity for me to meet them informally and—well, it's just too bad it had to fall on New Year's Eve."

Melora was silent for just a moment. "Of course you must do anything that will help you in your work. It's quite all right, Tony. We'll be glad to see you whenever you're free. Well—I'd better not keep the others waiting. . . ." She moved toward the door.

He made no effort to stop her. "Thanks for understanding. And of course I'll see you—soon. I— I'm so glad you could come tonight. Good night, Melora"

"Good night," she said and went out the door.

Out front the theater had emptied and stage hands

were pulling up the curtain on empty seats. It was as if she had somehow stepped into a new dimension where none of the old rules held. It was a dimension to which she did not belong. She had the feeling that she would not see Tony again except as strangers meeting.

She walked quickly to the stage door and down the steps that led to the street.

Quent and Cora were waiting for her on the sidewalk and she tried to smile at them, but in spite of herself her lips quivered.

Quent said, "We'll take a hack home tonight and travel in style."

All the way home he kept up a running stream of nonsense that reduced Cora to giggles. Melora sat in the dimness of the cab and said nothing. She was grateful to Quent. How had she ever thought of him as clumsy and insensitive? He was clumsy only when he chose to put on that old manner of his—something he adopted less and less these days. He kept Cora from asking any questions until they were home and ready to go upstairs to their rooms. Then Cora would not be stopped.

"What happened at the theater?" she asked Melora. "Tony seemed so odd. What did he say? Is he going to be able to get away in time on New Year's Eve?"

Melora answered only the final question. "I'm afraid Tony has to do something else New Year's Eve."

Quent stemmed any further outburst from Cora by flinging his hat in the air. "Hooray! Then you'll be my girl on New Year's Eve and nobody else's! Now you hush, Cora, and leave your sister alone."

Cora asked no more questions for the moment. The three tiptoed upstairs and separated to their rooms.

Melora was slow about undressing because she kept getting lost in long, puzzling thoughts. She sat with a stocking in her hand, trying to understand how she felt, trying to understand what had happened tonight.

Cora tapped on the door, and tapped again before Melora roused herself to a reluctant "Come in."

"Heavens, aren't you ready for bed yet?" her sister asked. "You'll catch your death sitting there mooning." She came in and threw back the bed covers. "Hurry into your nightie and I'll tuck you in the way you used to do me sometimes. Melora, has something gone wrong between you and Tony? Are you sad tonight, Mellie darling?"

Melora shook her head, though her denial wasn't quite true. She did feel wistful and a little sad over the loss of something that had promised to be lasting and lovely. Yet at the same time there was a sense of relief too because she would no longer be torn two ways.

"Some day, years ahead," she mused as she got into her nightgown, "you and I will sit in a theater watching the famous matinee idol, Tony Ellis. And we'll remember that once upon a time during the days after the fire we were both a little silly over him."

"*I* was certainly silly over him," Cora agreed. "But when that Mae Wentworth came in the dressing room tonight—well!" She turned off the light and her tone changed, brightened. "Mellie, do you think it would be all right if I asked Harry Norman to come to our party on New Year's Eve? Of course it's terribly late for an invitation and I suppose he'll already have an engagement, but—"

"I saw how he looked at you," Melora said. "I think he'll come if you ask him."

Something had happened for Cora too tonight. How strange a thing was this matter of "love." How easily you could be mistaken and how dreadful if you acted too quickly so that you discovered the truth when it was too late.

Cora tucked the covers up around her and dropped a quick kiss on her cheek. "Don't be sad, Mellie dear."

She hurried to the door and slipped out. When she'd gone, Melora lay against her pillow. A stream of moonlight came through one window, touching the figure of Kwan Yin almost as the stage spotlight had touched Tony and Mae. The blue coils of hair showed darkly, their color barely visible. The gold face gleamed like a smaller moon.

Blue hair, Melora thought drowsily. Quent liked blue hair. Quent was trying to help her. She was fonder of him that she'd thought. . . .

Suddenly she knew exactly what she would do as the final touch for her New Year's Eve costume.

21

A LADY
WITH BLUE HAIR

It was a good thing that Gran was knitting sweaters for the men of the household these days and there were those hanks of yarn in her work basket. She granted cheerful permission for use of the royal blue. Early New Year's Eve, so they'd have plenty of time, Melora went to work, with Cora's help, coiling and pinning and coiling again. When the task was finished Cora stood back to look her over.

"You don't exactly resemble Kwan Yin," she said. "But I must say blue hair becomes you. And with the blue color picked up again in the embroidery on your yellow gown—well, I think you're stunning."

Melora looked at herself doubtfully in the glass. Would Quent think so? In her wish to please him there was none of the anxiety she had always felt with Tony. There was simply the knowledge that she liked Quent very much and that she hoped he liked her.

When the two semi-Chinese maidens went downstairs together later, their descent was entirely as dramatic as any entrance Mae Wentworth had ever made on a stage. Harry had been happy to come, and he stood beside Quent near the big fireplace in the entry hall, his eyes popping with admiration. He looked very handsome as a Mexican *caballero*, with short jacket and tight trousers. But Melora liked Quent's outfit best. There was no doubt about what he represented. In those loggers' boots, red flannel shirt and battered top hat dusted with ashes, he looked like more than one refugee from the days of the fire.

He leaned against the mantel, watching both girls with that look that was so hard to read. Melora began to feel a little uncertain as she reached the bottom step and he still said nothing, made no move to come toward her. She put up her fingers to see if the blue wig was slipping, but all seemed to be well.

Now everyone came in from the parlor to see. Even Quong Sam opened the dining room door to have a look for himself.

"But you ought to have a gold face!" Alec told Melora, and they laughed.

"I'm sure you'll both catch cold in those robes," Mama said worriedly, but Cora assured her that they were wearing sweaters underneath, and Quent said they'd do so much walking there'd be no chance to get cold.

Sam scuttled to open the door for them and just as Melora passed him he whispered so no one else could hear: "You got mo' betta blains now, Missy M'lory."

Melora had to laugh a little as she went down the steps with Quent, though she wouldn't tell him what Sam had said. He still made no comment about her appearance, and she could only think that he had forgotten the remark he had once made about wanting to know a lady with blue hair.

It was nearly eleven by the time they reached Van Ness and the holiday crowd streamed along in full

force. The wide street was gay with lights. Waving
flags hung above the new redwood shops with their
freshly painted fronts. There was the gayety of re-
naissance in the air.

Up and down the street went the celebrants in
costumes of every description. Fillmore, Quent said,
was crowded too, and Golden Gate Avenue was used
as a connecting link between the two streets. There
were wigs and false noses and pasted-on whiskers
wherever you looked. A bedlam of fish horns and
whistles and cowbells served notice of New Year's
Eve. Quite a few police were out, but though the
crowd's excitement was intense, it was good-natured.

A clown with red circles painted on his cheeks
sprinkled Melora's blue hair with confetti and danced
away laughing. Bags of bright confetti were sold at
stands and Quent bought a supply so they could pelt
when they were pelted.

A sprightly oldster in the dress of a '49 miner stopped
them as they went by. "You young folks know what
happened today?" he demanded. "Ferry clock started
up of its own accord—that's what. It's an omen, sure
enough. This is gonna be the best dang city in the
whole U.S.A.!"

A court jester tickled Cora's neck with his feather
duster and tried to coax her to run away with him,
but nobody minded. It was all in good fun.

Yet while they pressed their way through the
throngs, Melora was very much aware of Quent,
moving rather soberly at her side. He tossed hand-
fuls of confetti and smiled at pretty girls, but he
seemed to be preoccupied with his own thoughts and
merely going through the motions. When a group of
merrymakers, clanging bells and tooting whistles,
separated the two couples, Melora and Quent were
pushed into an empty side street.

Quent called back to Cora and Harry, "You go ahead. We'll see you later."

Then they stood aside from the noisy crowd, catching their breath for a few moments.

"Why the blue hair?" Quent asked.

Melora smiled. "Don't you remember what you said one time about a lady with blue hair?"

"So it *is* on purpose? I remembered, but I didn't expect you to. I thought it might be just an imitation of your friend Kwan Yin. I want to talk to you, Melora. I didn't know if there would be a chance tonight, but this looks like an opportunity."

"But—what about Cora and—"

"They'll just think we couldn't catch up with them. We'll see them later at home. Talking to you is more important."

She walked along with him into the emptiness of the east. Ruins were coming down in this section, and near Van Ness new buildings had gone up. But there were still empty stretches on every hand where once city houses had stood.

A hackney cab jolted past on its way to a more populated section and Quent hailed it on impulse.

"I've an idea!" he said to Melora. "In you go!" and she climbed into the seat. "Nob Hill," he told the driver. The man shrugged, apparently thinking that you could expect almost anything from a fare on New Year's Eve.

"You goin' to the Fairmont, maybe?" he asked jovially. "They ain't quite open for business yet, y'know."

"Not the Fairmont," Quent told him. "I'll let you know where to stop."

"What are you up to?" Melora asked, feeling more and more curious.

But he would not tell her. "You'll see," he said and laughed at her bafflement.

The hack carried them slowly to the heights, zig-zagging along the streets to rest the horse.

"You can stop here," Quent directed when they were near the top. "Here's pay for the trip up. We'll be back in a little while for you to take us down and there'll be a tip for you if you'll wait."

The cabby agreed to wait, and Quent helped Melora down. He was looking less sober now, and his fingers were gentle about her own.

"Come along then, my lady with blue hair," he said. "This is a crazy notion, but I've always wanted to come back here. And perhaps New Year's Eve is exactly the right time for a view."

She remembered the Quent who had seated himself lazily on a wall on Telegraph Hill. That Quent had sometimes been a fake. Now he was no longer pretending anything.

She recognized the neighborhood. This was not far from the place where Alec had been hurt. They turned a corner, climbing, and suddenly she glimpsed what he had brought her to see. Shadowy white there on the hillside stood the marble columns of a door-way. A doorway to the past, Tony had said. But Quent had said it was a doorway to the future.

He went up the shallow steps ahead of her and turned to hold out his hand. "Come up here, Melora. I can't think of a better place to watch 1906 go out and the future come in."

In the starlight the mixture of the old and the new spread out below them. There were black patches of nothingness, it was true, but there were many more lights as well. A glow touched the sky from the direction where the New Year's crowd thronged Fillmore and Van Ness.

"We're doing it!" Quent said and there was an exultation in his voice. "We're doing what everyone said could never be done."

Melora felt tears burn her eyes, but they were tears of pride, tinged with only a wistful sadness for all that was lost and gone and would never come again. What was to come would be new and different and changed.

Quent searched her face in the dim light. "Do you think you could tell me about you and Tony Ellis?"

She blinked the moisture away. "There's nothing to tell. He's going in a different direction from mine, that's all."

"It's not all," said Quent, his voice a little hard as he spoke of Tony. "It's not all if you care a great deal because your roads are separating."

She looked off toward the glow and clamor of Van Ness and Fillmore. Was Tony somewhere in that crowd? And if he was, did she want to be with him? She knew the answer truthfully.

"I don't think it matters," she said. "Except—" she had to be honest about this if she could—"except with a little part of me that will always remember him."

"I can understand that," said Quent.

Somewhere a blare of sound began. Out on the bay ships commenced to blow their whistles, while all the fog horns snorted. All about them San Francisco—much of it seeming so dead and so dark—erupted into an ecstasy of greeting to the new year. Fire and earthquake were behind, an exciting future lay ahead. What else could you do but yell and whistle and pound your neighbor on the back?

Quent's arm came about her. "Happy New Year, Melora."

She looked at him, her eyes shining. But before she could repeat the greeting he bent to kiss her.

"The fire brought some good things," he said. "It showed me what Melora Cranby was like, for instance. Do you suppose a lady with blue hair could be persuaded to put on my ring again? And not in make-believe this time?"

His arms about her felt as they should. There was no doubting now, just this sense of deep and wonderful contentment.

"My finger has felt empty without it," she said.

He had it in his pocket and she knew then that he had planned something like this from the start. Even when he had looked at her so guardedly as she came down the stairs tonight, he must have had this in mind. He hadn't been sure then, had not wanted to betray his own feelings—had just waited to see.

The ring slipped on her finger as if it belonged. You could grow into loving a person almost without recognizing what was happening. Perhaps growing into love was the only sure way.

"There'll be a commotion when we go back and tell them," Quent said, laughing a little, remembering other commotions.

"But a pleasant one for once," she said. "Mama will be tickled pink and so will Papa and your father. Even Quong Sam will approve of me."

They went back to the cabby, drowsing on the seat as he waited for his peculiar passengers to return. Quent woke him and they got in, giving the address on Washington Street. They'd be going back to the supper party now, and they'd probably find Cora and Harry already there.

It was fun to be kissed again in the cab, and a little surprising too. Because Quent had been here all along and she hadn't looked his way. Yet now—

"We'll not have much to start off with you know, young woman," he told her. "The Seymour fortune is gone."

"We'll manage," Melora assured him. "We don't need Nob Hill. And I'll work hard at my writing.

After all, we're the new pioneers. And when did pioneers have things made easy for them?"

The cab jogged along toward home and into the year of 1907.